To Kaitlyn,

# LOGAN'S STORY

FORBIDDEN ROCKERS

SARAH ROBINSON

*Sarah Robinson*

**Logan's Story © Sarah Robinson**

**Copyright © 2014 by Sarah Robinson**

All rights reserved. This document may not be reproduced in any way without the expressed written consent of the author. The ideas, characters, and situations presented in this story are strictly fictional and any unintentional likeness to real people or real situations is completely coincidental.

This book is licensed for your personal enjoyment only. This book may not be re-sold or given away to other people. If you would like to share this book with another person, please purchase an additional copy for each recipient. If you're reading this book and did not purchase it, or it was not purchased for your use only, then please delete and support the author by purchasing the book from one of its many distributors. Thank you for respecting the hard work of this author.

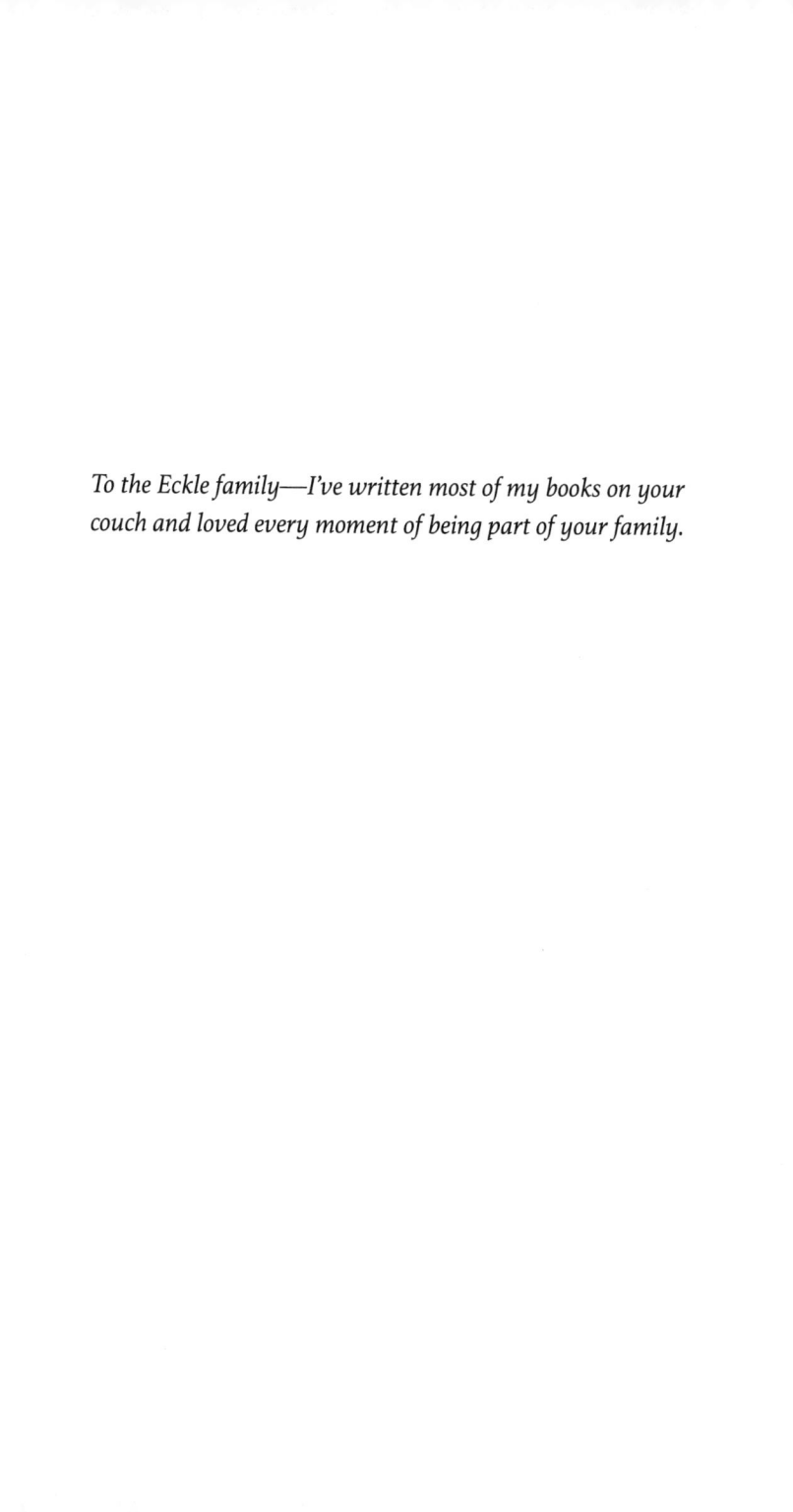

*To the Eckle family—I've written most of my books on your couch and loved every moment of being part of your family.*

## PROLOGUE

1994

My feet didn't even reach the floor. I just saw them there, swinging over the edge of the chair hopelessly, above the tile floor.

Dad's feet reached the floor. He was sitting next to me, his elbows on his knees and his feet flatly planted. I wondered if I'll ever be that tall, or if the only thing that will ever make me feel strong and big is the Superman cape I kept hidden under my pillow at home.

A tall man in pale blue pants and a shirt that looked like pajamas walked into the waiting room, pulling a white mask off his face. He was grimacing at my father, and then he looked at me.

Sadness? Pity? I wasn't sure what he was feeling toward me, but I knew I didn't like it.

My dad jumped to his feet so fast, the plastic chair he was sitting in almost fell over.

I jolted, startled at the sudden movement and wondering where he was running off to.

"Mickey Clay?" the doctor asked.

I waited, silently begging the doctor for good news.

"Yes, that's me. How is my wife? Is she okay?" Dad's speech was so fast, his throat scratchy and bumpy.

I'd only heard him like that a few times before, and the last time was Grandma's funeral.

"Laura is doing fine. She came through surgery well and is currently still sedated," the doctor explained. "We are going to keep her under to give her body and her brain time to heal. The trauma was severe. We're still watching her blood work. Her kidneys are showing some signs of strain."

I frowned, and I felt my brows pinch in frustration. I didn't really understand everything he was saying, but I knew what "fine" meant. She was going to be fine—my mom was going to be absolutely fine.

Dad still looked worried. "When can I see her? When will she wake up?"

"You can see her now if you want, but I have to warn you, she is hooked to several tubes and wires. It can look frightening." The doctor nodded toward me.

I stiffened at his warning. I was brave. Mom told me that all the time. I wouldn't be afraid of a few dumb tubes and wires.

Dad looked at me, too. "The boy'll be okay. Comes from good Irish stock. He'll handle it."

"When will she be awake?" Dad asked again.

"Let's see how she does overnight, and then reassess her vitals," the doctor said, looking back at the papers in his hands.

"I want to see her," Dad replied firmly, crossing his arms and jutting out his chin.

I held my breath, waiting.

After a moment of hesitation, the doctor nodded. "Of course. I'll have one of the nurses take you to her immediately."

I released the breath I was holding in one long exhale. I could see Mom. People usually gave in when his dad stood up to them.

"Uh, Mr. Clay, there is one more thing I need to talk to you about." The doctor cleared his throat.

Little lines formed around Dad's eyes as he stared at the doctor, and his entire body tensed. Seeing his reaction, I began to worry again, too.

"When your wife's car hit the pole, the car stopped, but her body kept going. Good news is she was wearing her seatbelt, which is the only reason she is still alive." The doctor sighed. "However, the bad news is the seatbelt held her bottom half still and the forward jolt of her top half broke several vertebrae in her lumbar and sacral spine." He avoided direct eye contact with me or my dad.

My heart raced. This was bad. It sounded bad. But he had said Mom was going to be fine? The doctor had said "fine." Tears pricked at my eyes.

"What are you saying?" Dad's voice hitched, confirming that things were bad, bad, really stinking bad. "Doc, are you saying my Laura is paralyzed?"

*What was para... paralyzed?*

"She won't be able to... walk?" my father pressed further.

*Of course Mom could walk. The doctor had said "fine."*

A frown creased my father's forehead, and he began to mumble softly. "We still go dancing every Friday night when we have a sitter. She waltzes around the living room when she vacuums for Christ's sake." He shook his head. "It'll kill her... just kill her if she's confined to a chair."

The doctor's face softened. "Nothing is confirmed until she wakes up and we run the necessary tests. But, you need to prepare yourself for this being a real possibility. She's lucky to be alive." He smiled at my father, but it looked fake, like the smiles strangers gave me when they wanted me to stop talking.

Dad stood frozen as he watched the doctor walk away. He looked...different. Nothing like the man who'd promised me earlier tonight that Mom would be there where when I woke up. She was a nurse and worked the graveyard shifts. He'd tucked me into bed, then gone back into the living room to watch the late night shows he loved.

I'd heard him get a phone call, laughing to whoever was on the other line. I knew it was Mom. I'd pulled under the covers and fallen asleep so quickly knowing Mom was coming home.

Only, she hadn't come home.

And the phone had woken him back up a few hours later.

Dad turned around to look at me, clearing his throat and blinking back tears. He glanced at my feet, which were now tucked up on the chair next to me. Normally he would have told me to put my feet down. He was always telling me to get my feet off the furniture.

He didn't say anything this time.

Dad shuffled over to me, taking the seat next to mine. "Son, you know your mama was in a bad accident, right?" His voice choked to a stop, and tears slid from his eyes.

I wanted to yell at him. *Men don't cry!* He'd told me that dozens of times. Men. Don't. Cry.

My dad was crying.

I closed my eyes so I wouldn't have to see his tears.

"It'll be all right, Logan," my dad murmured, scooping me into his lap. I collapsed against his chest and buried my face in his plaid shirt. "It's all going to be fine," he kept telling me as he carried me to the nurse's station. "We just have to find your mom."

# 1

2010

"Dude, you're bleeding." Dylan nodded his head toward my hand. "Damn, Logan."

"Oh, shit." I glanced down at my fingers. Blood was dripping onto the strings of my guitar. I propped the guitar on a nearby stand and stood up. "I'll be right back."

Dylan shot me an exaggerated eye-roll. "Don't get blood on the stage, asshole. Christ's sake. There's hardcore, and then there's hard-fucking-core."

I laughed, rolling my eyes as I headed to the tiny bathroom backstage. I was damn used to razzing from my band mates at this point, and they all knew well enough not to fuck with me too far. There was no way to explain to anyone who didn't live and breathe art, how much I loved the pain that came with plucking the chords of the perfect song.

A little blood was an easy price to pay for a melody that carries me away on its harmonies.

I grabbed the door handle for the bathroom, then immediately let go. *What the fuck.* Something sticky was on it. A gloppy, green substance now mixed with the blood from my blistered fingers. *Fucking pigs.* Another con of touring—

musicians could be gross as hell. It was like a freaking fraternity on steroids half the time.

Bypassing the handle, I moved to the faucet and shoved my hands under the not-so-clear water churning out of the pipes. The mirror in front of me showed the dark circles under my eyes from being up all night playing in dive bars.

*One day.*

One day I wasn't going to need these crappy gigs where the only people left listening at the end of the night were a few drunk groupies hoping to go home with someone in the band, or the career alcoholics who couldn't find their way to the door.

*Haven* was going to be big one day. I was sure of it. We had named the band after the town we'd all grown up in, but our eyes had always been set on New York City. We'd get there if I had any say in it—and being the lead in the band, I had all the fucking say.

Dylan was putting his instruments into cases when I walked back onto the stage, and our band members were already loading amps onto a cart to take them to the van.

I grabbed the tip jar at the edge of the stage and glanced inside to see three crumpled dollars and some coins. My jaw tightened, thoughts of the bills I needed to pay overwhelming me. They weren't even all my bills—in fact, the majority weren't mine. But I was still the one who needed to pay them.

Hell, my bandmates had just as many bills as I did and they were all depending on me. This was on me.

"How did we make out?" Dylan called out.

"We might be able to split one beer," I replied, emptying the contents of the jar into a bank envelope to distribute later with the fifty dollars the bar owner paid us for the night. "Maybe two."

Rock sighed, and Dylan and Charlie looked at each other in frustration, but no one said anything. We were artists first. It wasn't supposed to be about the money. And the truth was that none of us did it for the pay, but we still had bills and responsibilities. Hell, I knew about that more than anyone.

I handed the bank envelope to Dylan and grabbed my guitar case. "I'm going to head out, guys. See you Friday at McGinny's?" I pulled on my jacket and swung the guitar case strap over my head. "We go on at nine."

"Yeah, but get there early for sound check, Logan. We need to be on our game Friday," Dylan reminded me—not that I needed it. "That scout from *New York, New Music* is going to be there."

I turned back around to face Dylan. "I thought he wasn't coming?"

"Apparently his daughter is a fan of Haven and she changed his mind." Dylan grinned, clearly excited.

My brows shot up. "Seriously? What a stroke of fucking luck."

"All right, you caught me. She is mainly a fan of yours. But hell, we're part of *Haven,* too." Dylan tossed up his arms and looked at our two other bandmates, Rock and Charlie, who both started laughing. "Even if we're not swinging our dick on the mic." Dylan grabbed his drumsticks and did a rim shot to highlight his joke.

I grinned, waving them off and ignoring their stupid jokes. *Fucking idiots.* God, he loved them. This was his family.

\* \* \*

My car took a few turns of the key before it finally churned over and started with a deafening roar. Just another bill I didn't have the funds to fix right now.

I glanced at the nearby houses with their windows darkened, hoping I hadn't awakened any of my neighbors this late at night. Turning my body to look behind me, I slid my car out of the driveway. Once safely on the road and headed toward my second job, I pulled a CD out of the glove box. I needed something to pump up my energy before work, since I'd only just gotten home from the bar gig with barely enough time to change into coveralls and shovel a few peanut butter and jelly sandwiches down my throat.

The power button stuck, but I shoved it hard, waiting for the music to start playing and drumming my fingers against the steering wheel. A screeching and scratching sound suddenly pierced through the dashboard and the music dwindled to nothing more than static.

"Are you fucking kidding me right now?" I hit the dashboard as if that would make the ruined CD repair itself.

*Of course.* The only thing that would have made his mood improve was music and his piece-of-shit car wouldn't even allow that. Irritation grew in my stomach, swirling and forcing me closer to my boiling point. I hit the gas hard, not planning on wasting another minute in this heap of scrap metal than I had to.

When I pulled into my employee parking spot behind the large warehouse I spent most of my nights in, I tried to push my irritation away and focus on what I needed to do. Grabbing the back brace from my passenger seat, I wrapped it around my waist and pulled the straps over my shoulders, then got out of the car and strode for the back door.

Coworkers were milling around, all wearing similar support braces and reflective orange vests with hats and gloves, loading boxes onto eighteen-wheelers for deliveries going out that day.

"You're late, mick," Joey growled from behind the warehouse counter where he was marking packing slips. He barely glanced up at me.

I ignored his ethnic slur. *Fucking asshole.* "Sorry, boss. Gig ran late." I grabbed my time card and punched it through the slot, then replaced it on the rack.

"Like I haven't heard that from your sorry ass before," Joey grumbled.

I just put my head down and continued to the larger part of the warehouse, nodding to some of the guys on the to the last loading dock. I hopped into a forklift and shifted the gears, picking up a pallet of stacked boxes and hauling it toward the truck.

The job was tedious, and I hated it, but the paycheck was good. There were very few people who eagerly worked twelve-hour shifts beginning at three in the morning, so it's not like the company had much of a choice but to ignore his tardiness.

I was used to starting this early now, and then crashing in the afternoon for a few hours before heading out for my next gig or band practice. On my rare day off, I would sleep in longer, but then still spend the rest of the day playing my guitar.

Music was everything in my life, and even as I loaded pallets stacked with boxes onto a giant truck, I hummed our songs and reminded myself who I was...and who I was going to be.

## 2

"Dad, wake up." My father was slumped over in his favorite chair in the living room, fast asleep. I didn't normally see him this tired, but my mother had been having a tough week, and that often took a toll. "It's almost dinner time."

"I'm up. I'm up! What's for dinner?" He yawned and groaned as he pulled his body out of the chair. "You cooking?"

"Almost ready, but I only have a few minutes to eat with you guys before I need to leave for the bar. We have a scout coming to see us tonight from New York New Music, so I want to get there early for sound check.

I glanced over my shoulder as he walked past the kitchen. I knew he was heading to get my mother.

I returned to my original task of pulling the pasta off the stove. I spilled it into the strainer sitting in the sink and shook off the excess water before dumping the noodles back into the empty pot. Next, I opened a jar of pasta sauce I'd heated in the microwave, and mixed it into the pasta with a bit of seasoning.

When finished, I placed the bowl of pasta on the table then added a plate of garlic bread I'd prepped earlier. Within a few minutes, the dinner table was neatly—though humbly—set for three people.

I stifled a yawn and decided to add a little caffeine to my meal, snagging a can of soda out of the fridge and cracking it open. My father entered the kitchen, carrying my mother, Laura, in his arms. He sat her gently in her special chair at the table, and they both complimented him for the food.

It had been almost twenty years since my mother had been in a car accident and lost any functioning below her waist. The paralysis was only one of the resulting medical problems that the accident left her with and my father had been forced to quit his job in order to take care of her full time. Trips to dialysis and multiple doctors filled their days now.

The doctor bills continued to fill our mailbox. There was no insurance, no money to pay for a nurse, so my dad stayed home to take care of my mom, and I worked to pay what bills I could.

It definitely wasn't the average life for a twenty-five-year-old man, but my parents were everything to me. I owed it to them.

I sighed quietly before joining them at the table. *Stop feeling sorry for yourself.* These pity parties were not his usual go-to, but for some strange reason, the last few days had become a tempting rut to hide in. Considering what a big deal tonight's gig was, my nerves were on overdrive.

"Logan?" My mother reached her hand out to me, and I blinked back to attention. "Your hand, son?"

My father was holding his hand out to me as well, preparing to say grace.

I quickly took both of their hands and bowed my head.

It wasn't necessarily my cup of tea, but it made them happy. I'd do anything to make my parents happy.

"Dear Heavenly Father, we thank you for the food our boy has prepared for us tonight and pray you watch over him during his audition. We pray you bring healing to my wife and thank you for all you have done for our family. In Jesus' name, Amen," Mickey spoke solemnly, his eyes closed and his head down.

My mother and I echoed our amen and picked up our forks, hungrily devouring the food.

It wasn't an audition tonight, but I didn't bother to correct him. They didn't completely understand my music, or all the time I put into it, but they were supportive of me anyway. The Irish Catholic in us was a strict way of life—a trio bonded by our strong sense of love and loyalty. Nothing was ever going to change that.

"You sure you want to go out tonight, Logan?" My mother glanced up at me with her big, round eyes full of concern. "You look so tired."

"Don't worry about me, Ma." I squeezed her reassuringly. "I'm fine. Hell, I'm excited!"

"Watch your mouth around your mother," Mickey grunted, then shoveled a piece of bread into his mouth. "No goddamn cussing in this house."

I laughed at my father's ironic statement. "Sorry, Ma."

My mother just rolled her eyes and smacked my father's shoulder softly. "After thirty years with you, Mickey, I'm not a damn porcelain doll."

I grinned, then downed another forkful of pasta into my mouth.

Dad just rolled his eyes, grumbling beneath his breath. It was all just a rough exterior. My father was a giant teddy bear with a gruff outer shell, and though he liked to stomp around and toss around his weight, he would do anything my mother asked.

\* \* \*

WHEN I GOT to McGinny's, I realized I was the first from Haven to arrive. Since Rock and Charlie were the ones with the van and all our equipment, I decided to camp out at the bar and order a drink to soothe my nerves.

Tonight could change my entire life. We'd never had a scout come see us before. The pressure was...fuck, it was stifling.

Not to sound melodramatic, but in the back of my mind, I knew I couldn't screw this up. Sure, I wanted to be famous and live out the dreams of every musician out there—I mean, who didn't? But this was more than any of that. My family needed me to succeed. My mother needed this.

"Seriously? An Irish man drinking a Guinness? Wow, you're a real rebel, huh?"

I turned my head to see the owner of the sultry voice who was somehow also dripping with sarcasm. A tall, thin, rail of a woman squinted back at me, emerald green eyes flashing as she leaned against the bar. She was supporting her weight on one leg, sticking out her hip with her hand propped against it. It was an aggressive look, and everything about her screamed combative, and yet, inexplicably, friendly.

I turned back to my drink and grunted. "What's it to you?"

As hot as this chick was, I didn't have time for groupies,

and this girl's eyes were only saying one thing. She was a distraction, and I had no space for that in my life. I cleared my throat at the thought of her...distracting me...and took another sip of my beer.

She pulled a bar stool from a few feet over and slid onto it next to me. Her legs crossed, she pressed her knees against the outside of my thigh and angled her body to face me. Her eyes never left me even though I specifically made an effort to stare straight ahead and ignore her. In a brazen move, she reached across me and grabbed my glass right from my hand. Slowly and purposefully, she sipped my Guinness.

I narrowed my eyes, staring at her lips as my beer passed over them. My frustration and annoyance were morphing into...fascination, and undeniable attraction.

She finished off the rest of my beer entirely, tipping her head back and exposing her long neck. Her straight black hair fell past her shoulders, revealing streaks of neon pink, orange, green, and blue hidden beneath the black curtain

*Fuck.* That was really hot. And surprising.

She leaned forward, pressing her breasts together with her arms and whispered in my ear. "Thanks for the drink."

With a wink and a faint grin on her lips, she stood and started to walk toward the door.

I think my jaw was on the floor, because I had no idea what just happened or why I wanted nothing more than to follow her out of the bar.

A glance at the clock over the bar told me I still had a little time before the band would be here to set up. Standing, I pulled a few bills out of my pocket and tossed them onto the bar. I walked swiftly in the direction the mystery woman had gone and shoved the bar door open. Looking for her, I finally spotted her rounding the corner of the building.

I didn't want to lose her around the corner, so I shifted to a jog. *What am I doing?* I didn't know why, but I knew I wanted her, even if I didn't even know her name.

*Shit, I don't even know her name.*

I rounded the corner so fast, I almost collided with the object of my attention. My mystery woman was leaning against the brick siding, one long leather boot pressed against the brick below the hem of her short red plaid skirt. She wore a tiny black sleeveless top that barely covered her upper half, slivers of her flat stomach showing above the top of her skirt. Her head was tilted down, allowing her hair to cascade forward and cover her face.

I approached her slowly, watching as she fired up a lighter and dipped the cigarette between her lips into the flame.

"Nobody ever told you those fuckers will kill you?" I said in a low, ominous tone, approaching her.

This mystery woman might have some sort of hold over me, but I was taking back control. She'd gotten the best of me at the bar, but I knew what she wanted. And I knew what I wanted even more.

She glanced up at me and a flicker of desire slid through the deep, green pools of her eyes. She held the cigarette between two fingers, and smiled at me. "Nobody tells me anything. For their sake."

She grinned, her eyes turning a darker hue as she raked her gaze up and down his body. *Damn.* He liked the way she looked at him—hungry and wanting. He wasn't a stranger to women looking at him that way—his long, wavy brown hair and tanned skin, plus chiseled jaw line, and a body that most weight lifters would envy was easily a target for women's lust. But the way she looked at him? It was something more. It was ravenous.

"You owe me," I informed her, my voice a little husky as I grabbed her cigarette and tossed it to the ground. I put it out with the toe of my boot, then placed my hand on the brick wall beside her head, the other in my pocket as I leaned into her tiny frame.

"Do I now?" She cocked her head to the side. "For what?" The way her eyes lifted to mine, gazing up at me below thick black lashed...this woman was walking sex.

"The beer. And the attitude." I pressed slightly closer to her, growling my last statement against her ear. A soft rose perfume from her skin hit me, and I couldn't help but breathe in deep, savoring her.

Tempting. So fucking tempting.

A shudder rolled through her, and she pushed up on her toes, fusing her lips to mine. Softly, she slid her tongue across my lower lip as she kissed me.

I didn't move. Hell, I was a little surprised at her forwardness. My breath hitched, and then I couldn't refrain any longer. I wrapped my hand around the back of her neck and crushed my lips to hers, pulling her tighter against me. I wanted her entire body pressed against mine, slipping my free hand around her back and pulling her hips forward against mine.

A small moan passed her lips and she squirmed to get closer, twisting her fingers in my shirt and closing any gap between us.

"Name?" I grunted as I pulled away for a moment. I felt weird enough I was allowing myself a moment of zero self-control. The very least I could do is know her name.

"Gina," she said breathlessly, blinking up at him, a dazed expression on her face. "I'm Gina."

"Logan," I murmured against her skin.

Gina slid her fingers through my hair. "Nice to meet you."

I flashed her a teasing look. "You don't know that yet."

My warning didn't scare her off. It seemed to actually spur her on. She lifted her leg, gripping her knee against my hip. I couldn't stop myself from pushing her harder against the brick wall, letting my length press against her core with only our clothes separating us. Our lips were moving fast, devouring one another as if this would all disappear if we didn't hold on.

I reached up behind her and tugged her hair back hard, but she didn't cry out. She only moaned and pressed her hips harder against me. With her neck exposed to me, I let my lips explore every inch of her skin until I reached the neckline of her shirt. Not even thinking about where we were or the fact that anyone could see us, I let my teeth sink into the top of her breast, nipping gently and pushing even further south. Within seconds, I had her nipple between my lips and she thrust her hips against me as she moaned her pleasure.

"Well, this is fucking awkward," a voice said behind me.

I jerked my head up, turning to look at a grinning Dylan, failing in his attempt to keep an innocent expression on his face. Rock stood beside him snickering behind his hand, barely trying to mask his laughter.

I rolled my eyes and made sure my body blocked Gina's so they weren't seeing everything I'd just had my mouth on. She scrambled behind me, readjusting her clothes.

"So, you comin' to sound check, dude? Or do you have something else you need to check first?" Dylan continued his snarky commentary as he leaned around Logan to wink at Gina.

"Shut the fuck up and get out of here," I replied, putting

an arm protectively around her. "I'm comin'. You jackasses are the ones who were late. You expect me to sit there like a dick and wait for your sorry asses?"

"Oh no, you definitely found a way to keep yourself busy," Rock chimed in, earning himself a punch to the arm as the men headed back into the bar.

I glanced back at Gina, checking to make sure she was okay. Her cheeks were a bit redder, but she still looked as good as before. "Later?"

She nodded, her tongue sliding across her bottom lip. "Later."

With that, I followed my band mated back into the bar, stealing one last glance in Gina's direction. He felt a twinge of guilt for dropping her like that, pausing mid-make out and all, but he hadn't known how else to react. His band mates had never seen him with a woman before because of how busy his life was. He'd never been the type to hook up with groupies, and had always left those wannabees to them.

He didn't have the time to devote to flirting or dating. Taking care of his family and playing gigs took center stage, and all the drama that came with women just got in the way of that. *So, why the fuck did I just let this girl sidetrack me on this biggest day of my career?*

Dylan and Rock were already on stage with Charlie setting up their equipment when I walked in. They were literally gossiping like a group of valley high teen girls, telling Charlie everything they'd just witnessed.

"...just going to fucking town, man!" Dylan regaled Charlie with the story. "Didn't even hear us come up behind him!"

"Hell, at least we know he still likes girls," Rock joked, just as I caught up to them.

All three men burst out laughing. A few patrons looked their way then went back to their drinks.

"Why don't you assholes just shut up?" I hit Dylan on the back of his head then stalked over to my gear on the side of the stage and picked it up. "Stop busting my balls like a bunch of jealous bitches."

They calmed down eventually, and we began assembling our instruments and electrical equipment on stage, though they somehow managed to keep throwing out the occasional barb.

I purposefully avoided any eye contact with Gina, who was now sitting back at the bar, a martini in her hand. I didn't need a distraction tonight, not when the record label scout would be here. No one knowing what he would look like, but we were all on the watch for him.

Tonight was the night. This was my chance.

# 3

Haven's first set was only eight songs long, which wasn't nearly as long as it felt standing on that stage waiting for the scout. The bar was mostly full, and as it got later in the evening, the crowd got larger. None of us knew when the scout would be coming, but we'd figured we should save our best songs for later in the evening when the crowd was drunk and cheering on everything.

Not that we had to worry too much about the band, since McGinny's patrons loved Haven and we'd gained a bit of local fame around town.

"Take five, guys." I slipped the guitar strap over my head and placed the instrument back on the stand next to me.

There was nothing I owned that I loved more than my red Fender Stratocaster. It went everywhere with me, and I took care of it like it was my child. At this point, it basically was. It's not like I was close to having a real family of my own one day. Hell, women and children were the last damn thing on my mind.

Or at least, women were until a few hours ago.

"More like ten, bro." Dylan cracked his neck to the side.

"I need a beer. Or three." He slid his drumsticks into his back pocket and stalked off to the bar.

Rock was fast behind him, always eager to pound away a few drinks.

I briefly contemplated joining them, taking a deep breath and releasing it closely. I didn't want to be drunk on stage though, not with what tonight meant.

"Relax, man." Charlie slapped me on the back. "They play just as good hammered. Hell, maybe even better."

He was right. Charlie had always been the levelheaded one in the group. The guys were as nervous as I was about the scout, and a drink or two would probably only benefit them. I decided to join them for a drink.

"What'll it be?" The female bartender leaned across the bar, purposely showing off her cleavage. I pretended not to notice the way her eyes raked across my broad chest and large biceps, or how she paused a bit too long when she looked at my lips.

Despite the confidence boost at her interest, there was absolutely no part of me that wanted anything to do with her. Not even remotely my type. She looked like she dunked her head in makeup every morning, as in her face was literally a different hue from the rest of her body. *No thanks.*

"Jack and Coke."

"You got it, baby." She moved around gathering the ingredients, intentionally putting on a show with the way she wagged her hips and dipped her breasts low in front of me.

It was easy not to pay attention, since my mind was already running through the chords for the next song.

"Switching to liquor?" Gina was beside him, her melodic voice purring against his ear. She wrapped her arms around his waist and looked up at him, grinning mischievously. "I thought you were a Guinness man, Logan."

The bartender took one look at Gina hanging all over me and dropped the glass down on the bar with a hard thunk, then slid it to me. She tossed her hair over her shoulder and walked away.

"Oh, hey Gina," I greeted her awkwardly, pushing my arm down enough to detach her from my waist while pretending to just be reaching for my drink.

She visibly pouted and scooted around to stand in front of me. "You mixed some chords in the last song, you know," she declared, the purr of sensuality no longer in her voice.

*How does she know that?* I was genuinely surprised she had noticed my screw up, let alone had the brass to call me out on it. I tilted my head to the side to look at her, narrowing my eyes. "You think so?"

"I'm quite sure," she replied, one hand on her hip.

For the life of me, I could not figure this woman out. Something about her was so irritating. Like, I honestly can't ever stand her. And then, at the same time, there was something sultry and unexpected in her tone and demeanor that made my heart quicken when around her. She was absolutely obnoxious and unusually clingy, but when her eyes blazed into me, I could feel that spark in my very core.

Desire thundered through me at her defiance and spunk, and I knew without a doubt that I wanted her right then and there. *Fuck. This is going to be a disaster.*

"What's your point?" I replied slowly, not wanting to let on that she was getting under my skin.

She shrugged her shoulders and looked down at her hands, fidgeting slightly. *Were those nerves?* I was surprised to see even the hint of a soft side to her. "You're going to need to be better than that tonight," she stated simply.

It wasn't a question or an encouragement. She stated it like it was just a fact.

I took a step closer to her, narrowing any gap between us. She retreated another step, only to find the bar behind her. I stared down at her, my towering figure shadowing her, and felt a shiver course through her. I wasn't sure if it was fear or arousal, but it was all I needed to want her more than I could handle.

In a flash, my mouth was on hers, and she might have fallen upon impact if my hand hadn't already grabbed the back of her neck.

Placing my empty glass on the bar behind me, I used my free hand to press her lower back forward, crushing her against my pelvis. She responded instantly, snaking her tongue against mine and letting out a slight moan as she ground her hips against mine. I knew she was feeling how hard I was for her, and how badly I wanted to fuck her right there against the bar.

*This woman is going to end me.*

Common sense finally takes over and just as quickly as I'd captured her lips, I let her go. Gina's expression was surprised as I took a few steps back from her. We stared at each other for a moment, just trying to figure one another out. Trying to figure out what I wanted. And, fuck, all I wanted was her.

Stepping back into her, I wrapped an arm around her waist and pressed my lips against her neck. Kissing my way up to her ear, I growled against her. "Meet me outside after the show. You're mine tonight."

Even saying those words set my body on fire. I wanted to claim her. I wanted her to be mine and no one else's, and I wanted to take everything she was offering me. Every part of my brain was screaming that this was a bad idea, that I needed to stay focused on tonight, but I couldn't stop myself.

I wanted this colorful vixen, and I was going to have her.

* * *

Adrenaline ran across my skin, zipping through me as I stepped onto the stage. The heat of the lights warmed me, only further surging my excitement as I looked out over the crowd.

She was there. I could see her seated on a barstool off to the side, her chin in her hand as she propped her elbow on the bar. She winked when our eyes met, but I didn't acknowledge her in return.

I was in the zone, and there was no place for anyone beside me except my bandmates and my guitar.

The bar was filled with twenty-somethings, downing drinks and cheering us on. Their energy was only feeding us more as I moved across the stage, lead vocals on the microphone and strumming my guitar.

Scanning the crowd, I kept my eyes out for one person and one person only—the scout. He was sure to stick out in a crowd like this, maybe a little older, more professionally dressed. He wasn't sure who it would be, but there were a few men who looked like they could be him.

We were just finishing up our third song when Gina motioned to a man at the door then hopped off her barstool to head in that direction. A surge of jealousy hit me, and I cleared my throat in surprise. Was she seriously meeting another man here after what had just happened? The woman was a goddamn mystery.

Pulling my eyes away from her, I focused back on the microphone and announced the name of our next song, *Thief in My Bed*.

Smiling at the crowd, I masked my emotions immediately, introducing each of my band members and waiting for a few moments in between as the crowd cheered for each. Returning to center stage, I began belting out the first lines of the song as the band joined in harmony.

*Stole my heart just to throw it away,*
  *No explanation for the games you play.*
  *Am I just a Friday night to you,*
  *or are we going to see this through?*

My gaze drifted back to Gina as I sang about a past unrequited love. She was sitting with an older gentleman now, chatting away and motioning toward the stage. I knew she was talking about me from her body language, but I couldn't help but feel pangs of envy tear through him as he watched her eagerly look up to the older man.

*Who was he?* Irritated, I quickly chastised myself for even caring. With some effort, I forced myself to focus back on the crowd and the lyrics.

*Between our kisses, you said "forever",*
  *but behind my back, you laughed "never".*
  *So, I tossed the thief from my bed,*
  *but damn it all, you're still in my head.*

. . .

I FINISHED the chorus and then stepped to the side, pointing my hands at Dylan who immediately launched into a drum solo that had the entire bar on their feet in seconds. The rest of Haven cheered him on as he skillfully banged out a rhythm on his kit, sweat beading on his forehead as he concentrated on each hit.

He was oblivious to the screaming; I smiled as I recognized the musician's trance. Dylan Moore might be an asshole at times, but he loved music as much as I did, and that was what solidified our friendship.

Dylan finished with several slams on his cymbals and then he stood up, his hands in the air holding his drumsticks proudly as the crowd ate up his performance. The rest of the band immediately jumped back into the song and I grabbed the microphone. The energy from the audience surged through me as I sang the final lyrics to the song.

*EVEN IF I lock up my whole heart,*
  *you pierce your way in like a dart,*
  *now your reign of power's through,*
  *I'm not the one you'll come home to,*

*DID YOU HEAR, girl, what I said?*
  *No more damn thieves in my bed.*
  *Did you hear, girl, what I said?*
  *Get the fuck out of my bed!*

I SLAMMED my hand down on the strings with the last line

and yanked up the whammy bar, creating an amazing piercing sound that I knew everyone could feel in their bones, vibrating through their veins.

The rest of the band was on their feet with the crowd, whooping with their fists pumping the air. The crowd's reaction slowly filtered into my awareness—previously centered on only that last note—and I allowed myself a rare moment of pleasure to soak it in their praises.

Rock grabbed his mic. "Give it up for *Loooooogan Clay*!"

The bar walls nearly shook with the deafening noise. I grinned and raised one fist in the air.

I spotted Gina in the crowd, almost obscured by the bobbing heads in front of her. Her thin frame was taller than the average woman, and even some men, but the crowd still hid her well as people waved their arms and cheered. I couldn't even believe I'd been looking for her, or that I had even noticed her in the first place.

"You guys have been great!" I thanked the crowd. "If anyone wants a CD, we will be selling them in the back!" I pointed to a side table off the stage.

I unhooked my guitar and sat it down on its stand, then highfived my mates as we all congratulated each other on a great performance. Off stage and slightly to the side, I spotted Gina waiting for me.

A bright smile crossed her face, and her green eyes swam with excitement. Warmth and arousal coursed through me, and I didn't even question myself this time when I winked at her.

"Did you just fucking wink at the chick you were banging in the alley?" Rock started.

Dylan pointed at Rock as if to agree with his question.

Charlie smiled at me, a cocky look on his face. "Our little

Logan is falling in love," Charlie teased, smacking me on the back.

I shoved him away and raised my chin. "What the hell are you guys talking about? It's just a one-night kind of thing, maybe not even that."

"Yeah, sure, lover boy." Dylan chuckled as he worked on disassembling his guitar.

I rolled my eyes and stalked off stage, irritated. They had no idea what they were talking about. They were always with different women every night anyway, so what the hell did it matter what I did. I wasn't looking for anyone.

*So, why the fuck did I wink at her?*

# 4

"I told you that you could do better." Gina leaned against the wall at the end of the stairs off the stage. Her legs were crossed, showing her long silky skin traveling up to the hem of her short skirt.

I slowed on the last few steps as I approached her, feeling wary of this woman who was causing changes in me I didn't understand.

She had swept her black hair around to one side of her neck, showing off the neon-colored highlights beneath. There was a small red mark at the base of her neck and I felt my dick harden at the memory of putting it there.

"You like to be right, don't you?" I smiled, only slightly conceding, as I placed a hand on the wall behind her and leaned in to trace a kiss across her lips.

"Everyone likes things they're good at." She looked up at me under her long lashes, breathless from our kiss.

I leaned closer, inhaling the perfume she wore, and brushing my lips against her cheek. "Damn it, Gina, who are you?" I groaned softly in her ear.

Her smile widened, our faces inches apart. She kissed me softly this time, then bit my lip at the very end.

I groaned and raised my brow. "Feisty."

She grinned. "Come on, you need to meet someone!" She grabbed my hand, pulling me from the stage and into the crowd. Visions of the older man she'd been talking to during the show popped up, and I balked; I didn't have any interest in meeting any men in her life right now. Besides, I had to find our talent scout, whom I had yet to spot.

"Gina, I can't." I pulled back and stopped in my tracks, making her turn around to look at me. "I'm busy."

"No, you're not. Trust me, this is who you're looking for." She gestured her hand as if to wave away my concerns and then looped her arm around mine, pulling me forward again.

"Daddy! This is Logan." Gina came to a stop in front of the man she'd been talking to during their set.

*Shit, is she crazy? Meet the parents already?* I suppressed the urge to roll my eyes and run for the door, and instead, I shifted foot-to-foot, uncomfortable and unsure of what to do.

"Great to meet you, Logan." The man stuck out his hand, and I accepted the firm handshake. "That was quite the performance."

"Thank you, sir," I replied, looking between Gina and her father.

A slight pause halted the conversation, and then Gina's face lit up with understanding. "Logan, meet Garrett Vile. Daddy, meet Logan Clay. There! Official introductions over, I'm going to get a drink and let you boys chat." She grinned, then winked at me as she flounced off into the crowd.

Garret chuckled, watching his daughter go. "Gina's always been a bit headstrong, but I knew when she first played me a recording of one of your songs that I had to meet you. I'm from New York New Music, I think you heard I was coming?" He crossed his arms over his chest, assessing me.

*Gina's father is the scout? What the hell…*

"Oh, wow, Mr. Vile, it's an honor to meet you," I sheepishly offered. "I'm sorry, I didn't know the name of who would be coming from the label. I'm honored you liked the show."

Garret nodded, like he completely understood. "We like to keep a low profile until we hear a singer perform. Recordings never do justice to the real talent, nor do they show stage presence. Logan, you not only have exceptional talent, but you owned the stage and the crowd. That's the sign of a true star in the making. I want you to come to New York in two weeks and play for the execs. Here's my card, set it up with my assistant."

He handed me a small business card and patted me on the shoulder. "I'm going to take you places, son. Seems my little girl has a bit of a thing for you, though. Have to put on my dad cap when I tell you not to hurt her. Understood?"

"Oh, of course. We just met tonight. There isn't anything, uh…happening," Logan fumbled on his words, not sure if he was lying, because the truth was that nothing was happening…yet.

Garrett stepped back and the smile returned to his face. "I'll see you in two weeks."

"Yes, sir!" It took everything in me not to jump on him in a bear hug. "I can't wait to tell the band. They're going to be thrilled." I was still staring at Garrett's business card like it was my golden ticket.

Garrett's frame suddenly froze and I looked up at him to

see why. "Logan, uh, this offer is just for you. Don't bring Haven."

I blinked in surprise and glanced toward the stage where my friends were still packing away equipment. "Mr. Vile, sir...we play together. We always have. They're great musicians, and they're also my friends."

"They are good," Garret confirmed. "But, *you* are great. I only deal in great. And you can call me Garrett." He patted my shoulder, a look of what might have been compassion in his eyes.

"I'm going to have to think about this, sir. I mean, Garrett." I shifted my weight from one foot to the other and pocketed the business card. "That's...that's just a lot to consider."

"The offer expires in two weeks. You're either there or you're not. I won't be returning. Make the right choice for you, Logan. Not for Haven." Garrett finished with a nod and then turned and walked away, leaving the bar.

I continued to stand there even after Garrett had left. *What the hell was I supposed to say to my friends? My bandmates?* We were a team. We were Haven. Doing this without them felt...empty. It wasn't what I'd pictured. It wasn't the dream.

Gina glided up to me and slipped her hands around my waist. "My dad just offered you a chance at fame, but you look miserable. What's wrong?"

My eyes found hers as her words registered, finally realizing why she was at the bar tonight. This was all thanks to her. She'd brought the scout. She'd been his ticket to fame and...leaving everyone he loved behind.

It was his big break, but it felt...broken.

"Why do you look so down?" she asked softly.

"It's nothing." I shook my head. "I just have a lot of decisions to make."

Gina pushed up on the tips of her toes and brushed her lips against my jaw, pressing more kisses in a line toward my ear. "How about we get out of here and you let me make the decisions tonight?"

The instant flame that cut through my body brought me back to attention, and I stared into her dark green eyes, thick with desire. Smiling, I let her take my hand, swung my guitar over my shoulder, and headed out of the bar with her.

I wasn't ready to talk to my bandmates, my friends. I couldn't say goodbye without them knowing something was off. I couldn't face them.

Gina was giving me the out I needed. At least for tonight.

\* \* \*

I couldn't even wait for her to open her apartment door before my mouth crushed against hers. Gina fumbled with her keys, gasping between kisses as we fed on desire and excitement, unable to keep our hands off each other.

When she couldn't find the right key for the slot, she groaned in frustration and turned around to face the door and focus. Instead, I grabbed the key ring from her and located the only key that looked like a house key on it, and then unlocked her door myself.

Gina wrapped her arms around my neck and with a slight bounce, she wrapped her legs around my waist. I held her with one arm under her ass, walking us both into her apartment. I tossed the keys randomly into the apartment, hearing them hit the floor somewhere not too far away. Both arms tightly secured around this lusty woman, I pressed her as close to me as possible. I relished the feeling of her legs wrapped around me, my dick prodding at the edge of her skirt.

With one fierce kick, the apartment door slammed shut behind us with a resounding thud. "Bedroom?" I asked, trying to catch my breath.

She pointed toward a hallway to the right, and I immediately moved in that direction, entering her bedroom only a few seconds later. In the center of the room, a queen-sized bed awaited, draped in a plush, brown comforter. I barely paid attention to my surroundings, heading straight for the bed.

Grabbing her by the waist with both hands, I pried her from my body. She whimpered and tried to maintain her hold, but I tossed her onto the bed instead. On landing, she bounced once then threw her head back and laughed.

It dripped of sex, and the sound should straight to Logan's groin.

With a growing sense of desperation, my fingers worked my belt, finally managing to undo it and the buttons on my pants, letting them and my boxers drop. They pooled at my feet, and I kicked them off the rest of the way. Pulling my shirt over my head as I kneeled on the edge of the bed, I paused for a breath before tossing the shirt to the side.

"Oh, God..." Her eyes widened as she stared down at my dick. The smile on her face was unmistakable, and my dick responded at her attention.

Naked, I straddled her, taking in her dark black hair spread across the blanket beneath her. Unable to control myself any longer, I captured her mouth again. Her lips were warm and pliant beneath mine.

I reached between us and hooked my thumb into the waistband of her skirt, tugging until it slid down her legs, then I ripped it off with one pull and threw it over my shoulder. Sitting up slightly, I gripped the hem of her shirt next and slipped it over her head.

Laying beneath me in only her matching black lace bra and panties, she was one of the most beautiful things I'd ever seen. "Damn it, woman...what are you getting me into?"

She crooked her finger, motioning for me to come closer.

She didn't have to ask twice. I was happy to oblige. I lowered myself onto her waiting body, amused and aroused by the tremors that ran through her when I placed my mouth on her neck.

Pressing my thigh between her knees, I spread her legs apart and settled between. Her knees locked on either side of my hips, but she quickly leaned over and opened her nightstand drawer. Handing me a small foil packet, she ran her tongue across her bottom lip.

I groaned at the view, taking the condom from her and quickly putting on. Pressing against her core, I felt her pushing back against me, wanting more. Capturing her mouth with mine again, I plunged my tongue inside and we kissed like we were devouring one another.

When I pressed inside her, it was fast and forceful. One long thrust and I was buried to the hilt, filling her with every inch of my cock. She gasped and arched her back, pushing her hips against me to go deeper.

God, she felt fucking fantastic clamped around me, squeezing me for everything I was worth. Moving hard and fast, I slammed inside her eager body as we tangled together —a mess of limbs and lust wrapped around one another.

Her body began to tense and I knew she was getting close. Reaching between our bodies, I found her clit and pressed hard, fast circles over it until she screamed and arched against my hand.

"Oh, God," she gasped, her hands clutching my shoulders as she pinned herself to me. "I'm going to come..."

"Good," I growled back, nipping at the skin below her ear. "Come for me. Now."

She did exactly as she was told and pulsed around me as she shook and trembled, moaning her pleasure as her orgasm rocked through her. Mine was moments behind and I buried myself as deep as possible as my own climax slammed through me.

"Fuck." I grunted and slid down to the bed beside her, already feeling happier and calmer than I had in years. Maybe ignoring women the last few years had been the wrong choice, because one good fuck and I was already feeling like a million bucks.

Gina turned on her side toward me and traced her finger in circles across my bare chest. "That was amazing."

"Mmm," I agreed, closing my eyes for just a moment. It had been fucking fantastic, but that's all it was—fucking.

*Right?*

## 5

I slowly pulled my arm from under Gina's back, and she moaned softly. I froze, listening for signs of waking, but she went back to snoring lightly with her head against the pillow.

Crawling out of her bed, I searched in the dark for my clothes. Finding my boxers, I yanked them on quickly then felt around for the shirt and pants I'd been wearing for less than a minute before stripping them off.

In a few minutes, I was fully dressed and sneaking out her front door. It was almost three in the morning, which meant I had to go to work. I felt conflicted on leaving her asleep like that—I'm not the player type who leaves women alone in bed. But, I couldn't afford to miss a day of work.

And the truth was...I didn't know what to say to Gina.

Last night had been amazing, and I still wasn't sure if it was from riding the high of the performance on stage or the intoxication I felt when Gina was around. In less than twenty-four hours, my entire life had been turned upside down, and I was letting a woman actually get in my head.

I cranked up the air conditioning in my car as I backed out of the parking spot and headed for the warehouse. I'd actually be on time tonight, which was ironic considering how busy tonight had been. There was no need for a caffeine fix even—adrenaline still coursing through my veins. Though he wasn't looking forward to the heavy lifting and physical labor part of the job. Hell, what he and Gina had just done definitely equated to several hours at the gym.

I couldn't help smiling at the memory, the feeling of her silky skin against mine and the tremors that coursed through her body when I touched the most sensitive spots on her. For a woman so obstinate and controlling, she relinquished a lot of her power in the bedroom.

Still daydreaming about our nighttime acrobatics, I pulled up to the warehouse and grabbed my shirt and back brace from the passenger seat of my car. I glanced down at my phone, briefly considering texting her, but no doubt Gina was still sleeping. I didn't want to wake her, but I also didn't want her to wake up and think I was just another asshole who fucked and then fucked off.

I finally decided to shoot her a quick text to let her know I'd had to go to work.

"Logan? What the hell are *you* doing here?" Joey glanced up from his magazine, his feet propped up on the warehouse counter.

"I'm scheduled to work tonight?" I questioned, punching my time card in. "Right?"

"Yeah, but, damn, you're on time." Joey chuckled and went back to looking at his magazine.

"Don't get used to it," I reminded him, then headed further into the warehouse to get started. *Maybe one day, I won't need a job like this.*

# Logan's Story

I thought briefly about the offer awaiting me in New York City, but quickly pushed the thought from my mind. I couldn't think about that right now. I couldn't picture what it would do to my life—destroying it and fixing it all at once.

\* \* \*

Almost dinnertime and at the tail end of a long and sweaty shift, I could practically hear my stomach growling as I walked into the house. A strong, meaty aroma hit me instantly, and I floated toward the kitchen, breathing it in like a lifeline. Mickey stood over the stove, stirring a freshly cooked beef stew.

Mickey glanced at me and grunted. That was about as much conversation as I expected from him. There was a pride in the way he looked at me, though, and I knew he liked seeing me come home from work. The aches and pains after a long day on the job were a reward for hard work, he'd taught me. Or, as Mickey would say, *"the example of a life well lived."*

After all, Clay men didn't do lazy.

"Beer's in the fridge."

I gratefully swung open the refrigerator door and popped the lid to an amber ale, chugging it down. The cool sensation sliding down my throat was an amazing contrast to a twelve-hour shift in the heat.

"Where's Mom?" I asked, wiping the beer from my lips with my thumb.

Mickey began portioning the beef stew into bowls.

"Upstairs. She just finished bathing. Can you bring her down for dinner?"

I nodded, taking the staircase in the hallway two steps at a time and heading for my mother's bedroom. "Mom?" I tapped on the door with my knuckles and walked in.

Laura Clay was sitting at her makeup table, looking in the mirror and brushing her hair. Tears were slowly working their way down her cheeks, and she startled when she saw me. "Logan! Oh, is dinner ready?" She quickly covered her face to remove any evidence of her tears.

I wasn't so easily fooled. I was by her side in seconds, though I didn't say anything, just placing one hand on her arm.

She gazed at me with a loving smile. "Look at my boy. So handsome. So tired." She cupped my chin and tilted her head to the side. "I'm a burden to you."

"That has never been, nor ever will be, true." Nothing could be further from the truth.

She rewarded me with a smile but didn't speak.

I stood back up from where I'd been kneeling by her side. "You ready for dinner?"

My mother set her hairbrush on the table and took a tissue to dab her eyes. "Yep, I've been smelling it from up here. I'm famished!" She grinned, her mood apparently lifting.

I bent down, sliding one hand behind her back and another behind her knees, then scooped her into my arms and held her firmly against my chest. She had always had a very small frame, so carrying her was not taxing in the slightest.

"Thank you, Logan," she said softly, her arms wrapped around his neck for support.

"It's nothing, Mama."

She hugged his neck tighter. "It's everything," she replied so softly he almost didn't hear her.

After witnessing her tears, I silently made the decision that I would go to New York no matter what. I had to do this not just for me, but for her.

# 6

I groaned, lifting a particularly heavy box and placing it in the corner of an eighteen-wheeler trailer. Monday morning had come quickly, and the flurry of Friday night's excitement was already a distant memory.

I headed back onto the warehouse platform. I only had Sundays off due to my crazy work schedule, and I had spent all of yesterday at home asleep or with my parents.

My mother had had a particularly painful day, so I'd played the guitar and sang to her as she lay on the couch waiting for the aches to pass. She had always loved my music. It seemed to soothe her when nothing else could.

My father, on the other hand, had never been a huge fan of music in general. He was gruff and loved anything physical, or hard work. Anything that could toughen a man by beating him down. That's how my father had raised me, or tried, at least. The moment he'd met my mother, he'd softened—even though he'd never admit it.

But then the accident happened. I had been too young when it all happened. I barely remembered what life with my mom had been like before she'd been injured. From the stories I had been told and the old photographs I'd seen, or the way my father spoke about what they'd once been, it was clear that accident had taken more than just her ability to walk. For years, sadness had presided over our house, with all attempts to remedy it falling short.

Then, when I began to show an interest in music about a year after my mother's accident, my father had actually encouraged it, despite his feelings on anything creative. He'd told me it was my mother's genes shining through, and he couldn't think of a single problem with that.

So, my father had learned some basic guitar chords and taught them to me. He'd worked extra shifts to afford music books and a ratty old acoustic guitar purchased at a yard sale. Music quickly became the epicenter of our house, washing away the sadness, and giving me a dream for my future that I'd do anything to reach.

I would practice from the minute I got home from school until it was time for bed. My mom began to ask me more and more often to come play for her. It became a sort of tradition when I'd play for both of my parents in the living room after dinner. My father would softly caress her hair as she leaned against him on the couch but listening to me play the latest song I'd learned or written. It was the first time I'd seen them be truly affectionate since the accident, as if it had brought them back together.

They'd give me pointers at first, critiquing my more challenging pieces, but eventually they would just stop and listen. My technique became better and better, and soon I was every outplaying my instructors and music teachers. But I never once played for them, or for the way people would compliment my talent.

I played for her, for my mother. For the way the music calmed her on her most pain-filled days. The chronic symptoms would subside, even if only for a few minutes. I loaded another box, and worry flooded my stomach as I thought about my mother's illness. Days like yesterday were happening more frequently than before. I'd tried to get answers out of my father after every doctor appointment, but all he'd say was that everything would be fine.

Everything was *not* fine, and I could sense it.

Doctor visits were closer together now, and my mom's pain was more intense, her energy lower. My father could live in denial all he wanted, but I knew things were getting worse.

My boss walked toward me on the platform. "Hey, Logan. Want to work a double today? Jimmy called out."

I considered it for a moment, though honestly there was no way I'd turn it down. I needed the extra income since I was the one who paid the bills at the house, not to mention trying to chip in toward the medical bills which were growing every day. "Yeah. I'll do it."

The more I thought about our expenses and how much the medical bills were increasing, the more I knew I needed to go to New York. I had no choice. I couldn't turn this down.

*How do I tell the guys?* I walked over to the water fountain. Pouring myself a glass of not-so-cold water, I grimaced at the warm taste as it slid down my throat. It was better than nothing at least.

I'd been dodging my bandmates calls and even left my cellphone at home to give myself an excuse for why I wasn't responding. I knew I had to see them at some point, though. I'd text them to meet me at McGinny's later.

I had to face the music at some point.

\* \* \*

McGinny's looked desolate on a Monday night with only a few dedicated alcoholics filled one corner table and a few stools at the bar. I wasn't surprised. I headed to the far end of the bar, away from the other patrons.

I wanted the privacy tonight anyway.

A scruffy, middle-aged bartender walked over to me after a few minutes and poured me a Guinness without even asking. I nodded appreciatively, liking that the bartenders here already knew him so well.

A gust of warm air swept through the bar as the front door opened and Dylan, Rock, and Charlie plodded in looking tired from their own work shifts. I downed the rest of my beer and waved them over.

"Hey, man!" Rock slapped me on the back and sat on the barstool to Logan's right.

Charlie nodded at me and sat down next to Rock—always the quiet one of our bunch.

"Where the hell have you been, man? Been calling you since Friday. Were you banging that girl all weekend?" Dylan joked, slapping the bar as he sat down to my left. "Bartender! Round of Guinness' here for my boys! We've got some celebrating to do."

Dylan didn't give me the chance to respond as he began chatting with the bartender. That was fine with me. I didn't want to lie to my friends, but I also didn't want to admit why I'd avoided them all weekend.

Though Dylan's comments did bring Gina to the forefront of his mind. A warmth passed through my body at the memory of her touch. *I wish she was here now.*

The thought surprised me, creeping up so easily. She'd crossed my mind a few times over the weekend, but I'd done nothing about it. There was no room for a woman in my life right now, particularly a woman so closely tied to his scout. It would complicate things, and he wasn't about to do anything to ruin his opportunity.

"We *are* celebrating, right?" Dylan looked over at me, and I could make out the worry behind his eyes.

Rock and Charlie leaned forward, clearly eager to hear about the scout. I felt sick to my stomach at the excitement on their faces. I was about to steal their dreams and destroy Haven—not to mention my friendships with each of them.

"The scout loved the performance. He said Haven was great." That much was the truth, at least, even though I was omitting the rest. I took a few more swigs of my beer.

"Fuck yeah, we're good! The crowd was freaking the hell out on Friday! Did you see my drum solo? I thought my sticks were going to burst into flames." Dylan puffed his chest out then chugged the rest of his beer.

"Logan had the crowd going nuts, too. Especially with that last song." Rock nodded at me. "That was a good pick, man."

"Friday was the best we've ever done," Charlie chimed in. He sipped his beer slower than the rest of us. He'd never been much of a drinker, which was good for us because he was always the designated driver.

Dylan picked up his second drink the second the bartender dropped it off.

"What else did the scout say?" Charlie asked.

Damn, that was the question I'd been dancing around. I sighed. "The scout, Garrett Vile, wants me to come to New York next week to play for the other record label executives at New York New Music." I looked down at the bar and rubbed the back of his neck.

"Dude, that's awesome! We're going to New York, baby!" Rock pumped his fist in the air and high-fived Charlie.

From the corner of my eye, I caught Dylan narrowing his eyes as he studied me. He was picking up what I was really saying. "Rock, shut the fuck up. That's not what he said."

Rock and Charlie turned to stare at me.

Swallowing, I got off my stool and took a step back, trying to collect myself. "Dylan's right. They want *me* to come to New York." I looked at his friends, pleading for them to understand. "Alone."

Rock set his empty beer mug on the bar with a solid thunk. "And then you said we're a band, so it's all of us or nothing. We're *all* Haven. This is not a one-man show."

"I tried. Swear to God." I chewed on my bottom lip nervously. "And I haven't given them an answer yet."

"This is bullshit," Rock said. "Fucking bullshit."

"I *need* to go, guys," I continued. "I can't pass up this opportunity. You know how much I need this."

Dylan stood silently, his face expressionless.

"*You* need this, Logan?" Charlie's fists were balled at his sides. I'd never seen him angry before. "Like we don't?"

"There were four of us on that stage Friday, Logan. Haven is a four-person band and it has been for years. We aren't your fucking backup singers." Rock took a step forward. His hand slid along the bar and knocked the beer mug to the floor with a resounding crack.

I cast a wary glance at the pissed off bartender.

"Come on, guys. Logan's clearly made up his mind," Dylan said to the other band members and motioned toward the door. "Let's get out of here."

Still scowling, Rock and Charlie followed Dylan toward the exit.

"Tab's on you, Logan," Dylan called back.

I didn't mind. It was the least I could do, even if I really couldn't afford it. Sighing, I pulled my wallet out of my back pocket and threw some cash down on the bar, enough to cover our check and then some.

I was frustrated and could only think of one thing to do. I yanked my phone out of my pocked and typed out a text.

*I'll be there in fifteen. You better not be wearing anything.*

I stalked out of the bar and toward my car, replaying the conversation with my friends over and over in my mind. I'd known they would be upset but, honestly, I had thought they would understand. They all knew about my family. They were part of my family, even.

I knew it wasn't fair and that Haven deserved the chance as much as I did, but would any of them have turned an offer like this down? I turned on the radio, increasing the volume as I pulled out of the bar parking lot.

A buzz came from my pocket, and I paused for a moment to read the screen, smiling when I saw her response.

*The door's unlocked.*

# 7

I definitely broke at least three or four traffic laws to get to Gina's townhouse. When I found a spot to park, I climbed out of my car, jogged up her front steps, then swung her door open confidently, as if I'd been there a million times.

Closing it behind me, I started shedding clothes as I walked to the bedroom. I wanted to forget all about what had happened tonight. I needed to be with someone who made me feel like a different person, like I could be more than I ever was. Being with Gina was a window into a life I could only dream of living.

I came to a complete halt when I reached the entry to her bedroom. Gina was stretched out across the bed, laying on her stomach and facing away from me. She was propped up on her elbows, reading a magazine, one leg lying flat behind her while the other was bent and dangling in the air above her. She was, as requested, entirely naked with only her jet-black hair splayed across her back, its hints of neon colors poking through.

I dropped my shirt onto the bedroom floor, making a

small sound as the fabric hit the hardwood. Gina glanced over her shoulder nonchalantly and smiled. Her gaze followed his, and he knew she'd seen him ogling her backside. She flipped over onto her back, leaning up on her elbows, studying him while allowing herself to be on full display.

My body responded and I groaned at the way her breasts swelled and her nipples stood for me.

"Stop right there, mister!" she said firmly.

Surprised, I paused. "What's wrong?"

"You can't just burst in here and take what you want." She smirked and tilted her head to the side. Her hair fell around her shoulders like a curtain. "I'm not a booty call."

"That would sound a lot more convincing if you weren't completely naked right now." I grinned, purposely pressing her buttons.

She huffed and made a pouting face. "Should I get dressed, then?"

"Don't you dare." I let out a low growl, rumbling from the back of my throat.

"You left before I woke up. I haven't heard from you since." Her eyes narrowed. "How do you think that made me feel?"

I tried to refrain from smiling because she actually looked fucking adorable when she was angry. Her nose scrunched up and her cheeks flushed red. I wanted to see if any other parts of her blushed as well.

I climbed onto the bed, sending Gina scurrying backward. I was faster than she was and easily pulled her toward me, pinning her to the bed beneath my body.

"I thought about you." I lowered my voice to a whisper, brushing my lips against her jaw and kissing her skin softly. "More than I'd like to admit."

"Really?" There was a quiver in her voice. She pressed her hips up against mine. "You thought about me?"

"Fuck yes." I groaned into her ear, running my hand down her side.

"I don't know if I believe you. I think I need some convincing," she said, a small smile on her face as she turned her head away from me in dramatic fashion.

I gently bit down on her shoulder eliciting a yelp. Then I lifted her with one hand behind her back and slid her higher on the bed, pressing her legs apart and crawling between them. I slid one of her legs up until her knee was bent and her thigh against my cheek. I licked the sensitive skin, alternating between nibbling and kissing.

She squirmed and tried to pull out of my grasp, but barely trying. Her breathing was ragged, and her skin damp —she wanted everything I was offering.

I gripped her hips, firmly pushing her into the bed and holding her still. "Stop moving and let me convince you," I ordered.

She giggled, and then dropped her head back down on the mattress. Her hips bucked against me as I moved my mouth from her inner thighs to her core. The moment my tongue slid against her clit, she nearly bucked off the bed.

I didn't let her move, though. Gripping her hips, I licked, kissed, and nipped every inch of her until she was writhing beneath me. My tongue plunged inside her, loving the feeling of her shaking and trembling around me as she reached her peak.

"Oh, God...Logan!" Gina cried out, grabbing my shoulders. Her nails dug in, but that only turned me on more.

When she calmed down, I moved up her body and captured her lips with mine. Leaning back briefly, I grabbed a condom from my pocket and put it on, then shook off my jeans. I climbed between her legs and pressed myself to her core.

"I need you..." Gina moaned, gripping my ass and pulling me against her.

I didn't need to be told twice. I thrust my cock inside her, loving the way she gasped at my intrusion. She wrapped her arms around me, holding on as I fell into a rhythm. Pumping into her, I growled against her neck, licking my way down to her breasts.

Circling my tongue around her nipple, I pulled it into my mouth and sucked hard. Her head pushed back into the bed as her eyes closed, her chest heaving harder as she panted with pleasure.

"I'm going to come again," she breathed.

I could already feel her pulsing around me and I knew she was close. Truth was, I wasn't far behind. She felt damn near perfect, and I wanted to bury myself to the hilt and pour myself inside her.

She moaned harder and began to tremble as her climax hit her. I thrust harder, meeting her orgasm with my own as I pounded into her and let my body release. God, it was exactly what I needed. The way she clenched around me, her nails scraping against my back as she moaned against my chest.

When we were finished, I fell to the bed next to her. She cradled into me, and I let her. I'd never been a very affectionate person before, but I wrapped my arm around her and pulled her tighter against me.

She sighed, and it was the happiest sound I'd ever heard. I smiled, knowing I'd been the one to give that to her.

\* \* \*

"Fuck them," Gina said, her head leaning against my shoulder. "*You* were the reason every person in that bar was on their feet cheering, Logan. Not your friends. Not Haven. If they can't be happy for you, then screw them."

I stared at the ceiling, unsure how I felt about it all. She was right, but I was also immediately defensive of my friends. "It doesn't mean they aren't happy for me. We have always been a band, and we always expected to be a band. I never thought once about going off on my own."

Gina sat up, leaning on her elbow and looking down at me. "Maybe that was before, but...Logan, you've outgrown Haven. *You're* the talent. You carried that show. My dad has wanted to sign you since I first told him who you were."

I glanced at her, my brows furrowed. "You were the first one to listen to the demo I sent in?"

Gina blushed, her cheeks turning red before she abruptly laid her head back down on my shoulder. "Well, yeah. It wasn't going to go anywhere since it was in the slush pile. But, I'd heard of you before, seen you play, and I wasn't about to let your demo go unnoticed."

I turned over on my side and pulled her closer to me. "Thank you," I whispered, leaning down and kissing her gently.

I loved the feeling of her soft lips, and I immediately wanted more. I gripped her hips, pushing her harder into the mattress as I rolled my body over hers. She moaned into my mouth and her hips moved against me. I reached between our bodies and slid my fingers across her wet slit.

She gasped and arched her back beneath me, but I didn't let her pull away. I teased her until she was writhing beneath me, groaning against my neck as she buried herself against me. When she'd completely unraveled against me, I pushed apart her knees and settled myself in between.

After quickly pulling on a condom, I buried myself in her in one long stroke.

"Logan!" Gina gasped, grabbing my biceps and anchoring herself to me.

"God, you feel so good," I whispered into her ear, then kissed down her neck until I reached her breasts. I took a nipple in my mouth as I continued to thrust into her. She moaned as my tongue flicked across her nipple, sucking softy.

"I'm so close." She panted.

I smiled, loving that I could get her there twice in a row. I was just as close and it only took a few more thrusts before we were both falling apart around one another. I groaned and bit her shoulder as I sank in as deep as I could as I came.

Heavily breathing, I slid to her side, keeping her pulled against my chest. "God, Gina...I don't think I'll ever get enough of you."

She sighed happily. "Good."

8

"Do you have to leave?" Gina pulled at my arm in an attempt to get me back in bed.

I grinned at her pouty expression and sleepy eyes. Leaning down, I planted a kiss on her lips. Her hands wrapped around my neck as she deepened our kiss, moaning into my mouth as the tip of her tongue ran across my lips. I had to pull back, even though I badly wanted to jump back into bed and ravage her.

"I wish I could stay, babe, but I have to go to work." I finally pulled himself away and grabbed my shirt off the floor.

As I yanked the shirt over my head, I looked back at the woman curled up in the sheets. One of her long legs was stretched out across the bed. The sheet barely covered her breasts. The sight of her naked body was intoxicating, even though I had already indulged myself more than once tonight. "You are making this so hard."

"Is that the only thing that's hard?" She giggled and threw a pillow at me where I was standing in the doorway, but I ducked and laughed.

"You are trouble, woman." I winked at her then headed for her front door, carefully locking it behind me.

As I walked to the car, I thought about everything that had happened between Gina and I. It seemed like just sex... but it wasn't. And it didn't feel like it. I couldn't get enough of feeling her against me, even just cuddling with her. We hadn't just had sex all night, either. We'd talked about our lives, our friends, my future. She was probably one of the most supportive people I'd ever met. She'd awoken something in me I'd forgot existed...and it didn't seem to matter that it was only our second night together.

Something about her beside me just felt right.

I stayed lost in these thoughts the entire way to work, still shocked about how much had changed in only the last few days. I was now thinking about a future with a woman I'd only just met, and a solo career I hadn't even known I could have.

I was being given a chance to become everything I'd ever dreamed of, to take care of my family financially, and to maybe even find love with Gina on top of everything else. It was like my life was finally falling into place.

I couldn't stop smiling even as I walked into the warehouse office to punch in.

"You're ten minutes late, Clay," Joey barked at me from his usual spot behind the counter. "Thought you were going to start showing up early."

I rolled my eyes, wondering if his ass was permanently glued to that chair. "I told you not to get used to it."

*Don't get used to me being here forever either.*

* * *

# Logan's Story

WITH MY TRIP to New York only being a few days away, my anxiety was on overdrive. Everything was just like clockwork, waiting for the days to pass. Working during the early mornings and all day, dinner with my family, practicing in the evenings, and then heading over to Gina's to spend the night tangled up in her sheets.

Whatever I'd begun feeling during the first few days I'd known her had only intensified. I loved spending time with my parents, especially playing guitar for my mother after dinner, which I never cut short. However, I couldn't seem to stop myself from eagerly awaiting the moment when I could leave for Gina's. Having her in my arms again was all I could think about—and I really needed my focus elsewhere right now.

As much as I wanted to focus only on New York and prep for the trip, I needed to find a way to calm my nerves. Spending time with Gina did that and more. Normally, I would have gone out for a beer with my friends to destress, but no one was answering my calls or texts, and I hadn't spoken to them since the argument at the bar.

So, almost two weeks later with only one day left before my trip to New York, I was shocked to walk out of work and see Dylan standing next to my car.

Dylan crossed his arms over his chest, leaning back against my door. "What the hell are you doing here, Logan?"

*What?* I looked at Dylan in confusion since he was the one out of place here, not me. "Uh, I work here?"

I tried not to sound irritated, but I was. All of my best friends had bailed on me during the most exciting time in my life, and then Dylan just pops up like nothing happened? Dylan and I were the closest out of everyone in the band. We'd grown up together and were like brothers.

I shoved past him and opened the driver's side door.

"I went to your house this morning to talk to you," Dylan explained. "Your dad told me you'd be done with work around now, so here I am."

I was waiting for him to get to the point, but he seemed to be hedging. I crossed my arms over my chest. "You know I always work Wednesdays."

Dylan kicked at the ground, shoving his hands in his pockets. "Would have thought you'd quit this place by now or been home practicing for tomorrow."

Guilt pricked at me again. "It's not a sure thing, Dylan. It's just an audition."

"It's a sure thing, Logan." Dylan lifted his head, smiling. "They would be idiots to pass you up."

My steely resolve softened. "That means a lot, man."

He shrugged nonchalantly. "No worries."

That was it. We were friends again. We'd never needed more than a few words, because our friendship ran too deep. I felt lighter, and relief poured through me.

"Want to come over for dinner?" I asked. "Dad is grilling tonight. I can just have him throw on an extra burger."

"Sure, I'm starving. Plus, I took the bus here, so I could use the ride." Dylan walked around to the passenger side and opened the door.

I laughed. "Ah, so the real reason for the surprise visit comes out."

"What I wouldn't do for a free ride," Dylan kidded.

We both climbed into the car, and I opened the middle console and grabbed my cell phone. I normally left it in my car since I wasn't supposed to have it with me at work.

"Shit!" I sat up straight as I stared at the screen when my

phone turned on and began beeping like it was about to explode with how many messages were coming through.

Dylan turned to face me, waiting for an explanation.

"My Dad's called me one, two...*nine* times in the last hour," I said, counting the missed calls.

"What? I just saw him a few hours ago." Dylan looked as nervous as I felt.

I was already dialing and quickly held the phone up to my ear, waiting for my dad to pick up on the other end.

"Hello?" His voice rang through the other end of the line, a slight panic hinted in his tone.

"Dad, I just got out of work and saw a bunch of missed calls. What happened?"

"Logan, it's bad. Your mother's kidney is failing. Come to Summit Memorial Hospital as soon as you can."

I groaned, dread settling in my stomach. She only had one kidney, and if she lost that one...fuck.

My father continued, "I don't know what is happening. They're doing emergency dialysis and running a whole fuck load of tests."

"Don't worry about anything, Dad," I assured him. "I'll be there in fifteen minutes, okay?"

"Hurry, Logan."

The line went dead, and I looked over at Dylan. He must have heard everything, or at least enough to understand what was going on. His eyes were wide, and his expression matched the panic I was feeling inside.

"Well, what are you waiting for?" Dylan urged. "Go. Now!"

"You're okay with coming with me?" Logan said, pushing his phone into his pocket. "I don't have time to drop you elsewhere."

"Drive," Dylan instructed him firmly.

## 9

"Every damn hallway looks the same." I rubbed my hand across my brow, attempting to calm myself.

The visitor's desk in the hospital lobby had sent him to the second floor, but I hadn't listened long enough to catch the room number since I'd been rushing to get up here.

"All hospitals are like that, man. Let's just find the nurse's station and ask them which room she's in." Dylan pointed back toward the direction they had just come from.

I nodded and followed him.

"There it is." Dylan headed straight toward the station after a few more turns and changes of hallway. He caught the first nurse's attention immediately. "Laura Clay. I'm trying to find the room Laura Clay is in."

The nurse looked at both of us for a moment, then sat down in front of her computer and typed a few words in. "Let me look her up." After a minute of me tapping my thumbs on the counter and shifting my weight from one leg to the other, she finally had an answer. "Room 207, hun. That's right down this hallway and to the left."

"Thank you!" I shouted back, already halfway down the hallway with Dylan close at my heels.

We came to a screeching halt in front of her room and stared at the curtain pulled across the door. I glanced at Dylan who gestured for me to go first into the room. I took a deep breath and pulled aside the curtain just enough to slip through.

Mickey was sitting in a chair next to the hospital bed. He put his index finger to his mouth, indicating for me to stay quiet.

My mother was fast asleep, curled into the starched hospital blankets. She was paler than when I'd last seen her before she went to bed last night and her hair was pulled back tightly into a braid. There were tubes and needles in both of her arms attached to large dialysis machines. She had other types of monitoring patches and clips on her fingers and chest as well as a nasal tube pushing oxygen into her lungs.

I was no stranger to seeing my mother in a hospital bed. She'd had dozens of stays since I was a boy, but somehow, this was probably the worst she'd looked since her original accident. She'd been on dialysis multiple times a week for years, still ranking way too low on the transplant list for a new kidney.

I could easily remember what she'd looked like bruised and battered after her accident when she'd lost her first kidney. I'd been so afraid at such a young age, worried I was going to lose my mother entirely. Now here I was, a grown-ass man, still just as afraid.

"What happened?" I whispered, crossing the room to join my father.

He stood and patted me on the back. "She passed out,

and I couldn't wake her so I called 911." Mickey sighed and shook his head. "Her remaining kidney is failing, son."

"But...the dialysis?" I asked. "She'd been doing fine."

Mickey shrugged his shoulders, looking more defeated than I had ever seen before. "We always knew that wasn't a permanent solution."

I put my hand on his shoulder, probably one of the more affectionate gestures we had ever shared, but it felt right. "Do the doctors have a plan? What are they going to do?"

He nodded, though he didn't look like he had any faith in their actions. "They're going to try a few things, like continuous ambulatory peritoneal dialysis. Some other medications. But, really, it's just temporary solutions. She has no working kidney." He pointed to the dialysis machine. "That damn machine is her kidney."

"How is she ranking on the transplant list?" I asked, even though I knew that she'd been a long way off for years.

Mickey sighed. "She's on it, but nowhere near the top. The machine is keeping her alive just fine, so they don't consider it urgent."

"Not urgent?" I could hear my voice raising, anger coursing through me. "She has to stay hooked up to that machine?"

"It's not the worst thing, Logan." My mother's voice rose softly from the hospital bed.

Both my father and I startled. Neither of us had realized she'd awakened, and we glanced at one another, unsure of how much of our conversation she'd heard.

I pulled a chair over to her bedside, sitting down and taking her hand in mine. "Mom, how are you feeling?"

Mickey rounded the other side of her bed and brushed a few small hairs off her forehead. "Hey, sweetheart."

"I'm feeling fine. Just decided to take a vacation." She let out a small chuckle, but quickly wheezed at the exertion.

I attempted a smile at her joke, but I couldn't. She never wanted anyone to worry about her, which was ironic since her health concerns made that impossible. I wanted to give her that ease, but I couldn't hide my worry. Not when things were so perilous.

"Aren't you supposed to be getting ready for New York? You have that big audition in the morning," she continued, squeezing his hand. "I wouldn't want you to miss it for anything."

"Mom, don't worry about that," I replied, leaning against the bed and propping myself up on my elbows. "I'm not going."

Mickey's head snapped up and he stared me down. "What do you mean you're not going?"

"You have to go, son," my mother insisted. "I've been looking forward to hearing you tell me they're going to give you a record deal and make you famous."

I shook my head, daring them to argue with me. "None of that matters when you're sick. I need to be here. Plus, there's no guarantee the audition will lead to anything. You need me here," I repeated firmly.

"Years of practice, dive bar gigs, expensive lessons...and you're not going to show up for the biggest day of your career?" Mickey was incredulous—or angry. I couldn't tell which. "You are our son and *we* should be helping *you*. Not the other way around, dammit." Tears shimmered in my father's eyes, and I almost couldn't believe what I was seeing.

My mother placed a hand on my father's forearm, gently comforting him.

In my entire life, I had never once seen a tear in my

father's eye. Not even when my mother first had her car accident. He was always composed, a man of few words. He grumbled and cussed, but he didn't get emotional. And he never, ever cried. Knowing I was causing this was filling me with a level of guilt I hadn't even known existed.

"Just...just fucking go." Mickey rubbed his temples with his fists, then stormed out of the room.

Stunned, I slumped in the chair next to my mother's bedside. "What the hell?"

"Your father..." My mother sighed. "He's going through a lot right now. He's a prideful man, and he doesn't want to admit that he needs you. That *we* need you."

I crossed my arms over my chest. "Well, whether he wants to admit it or not is fine. I'm staying."

"Logan, if you really want to give me what I need—what your father needs—you will leave." Her voice was a bit shaky. "What I need is to know that I didn't hold you back. To know my son lived his dreams." She took a deep breath as if the entire exchange was exhausting her. "What I need is for my son to take one day out of his whole life and do something for himself."

"Mom, I don't need—"

She cut me off as she continued, "I don't want to be a burden on anyone, Logan. Your father doesn't want to have to depend on you either, even though so often we have to."

As my mother's words soaked in, I began to realize how powerless my father must feel. Not only can he do nothing to heal the woman he loves, but then he also has to lean on his son for both financial and emotional support.

"Logan, I just want you to be happy," his mom concluded, her eyes pleading with him. "And that's not going to happen at my bed side and working to make the bills meet each month."

I took her hand in mine again, kissing the back of her palm. "I am happy, Mom. Nothing makes me happier than being here for you."

She shook her head, not buying a second of it. "You're not happy loading boxes in a warehouse and then coming home and changing my bed pans.

"Mom—"

"That look you get on your face when you play," she interrupted. "That's your heaven. And…and it's mine. I need that look on your face, Logan. It fills me with joy to see your face when you play. The entire world needs to see that, too. Please do this. For me?"

She spoke with such conviction, her voice getting stronger with every word, that I knew I couldn't deny her this request. I leaned in to kiss her on the cheek. "I'll only be gone one day and then I'm coming right back."

She smiled. "Maybe they'll find a transplant by the time you get back. There will be nothing to worry about."

I highly doubted that, but I wasn't going to tell her that. "I'm going to go find Dad." I stood and headed toward the curtain enclosing the room.

"Thank you, Logan," she said, a satisfied look on her face.

And really, that smile was all I was doing this for anyway.

\*\*\*

I EXITED my mother's hospital room and headed down the hallway to the waiting room Dylan and I had passed on our way in. I figured Dylan had probably run into my father and they'd gathered there.

A vibrating in my pocket pulled my attention, and I picked up my phone. A smile crept on to my face when I saw Gina's name lighting up my screen. *I miss her.* The thought caught me completely off guard, but it wasn't frightening. In some strange way, it was comforting. She felt like she belonged as part of my life.

G: *Hi, handsome. Coming over tonight?*
L: *Mom's sick. At Summit Memorial. Headed home to pack in a few.*
G: *Is she okay? Do you need anything?*
L: *Long story. I'm good.*
G: *Logan, what do you need?*
L: *Come to NYC with me.*
G: *Packing now.*

I GRINNED AT HER RESPONSE, relief sweeping over me knowing that I'd have her by my side for one of the biggest moments of my life. The way she was through my choppy messages, knew I needed her...it was special. She was special.

It was becoming more and more clear to me that I needed her...in more ways than one.

"How's your mom, dude?" a familiar voice said when I rounded the corner into the waiting room.

I looked up from my phone, pausing mid-stride for the second time today. I pressed my lips together tightly and looked around the room at the scene in front of me. Charlie had been the one to speak first, standing next to Rock and

Dylan, who were all getting up out of their chairs and coming over to him.

Speechless, I hung my head, shaking it slightly. I wasn't sure I could talk without choking up, and that certainly wasn't something I'd ever done in front of my friends before.

"Aw. We made the kiddo cry," Rock teased with a small jab to my upper arm.

"Buck up, man." Charlie jumped in on the banter. "You can't be puffy eyed for your big audition."

I laughed, the lump in my throat dissipating as their jokes eased the tension in the room.

"I didn't call them, man. I swear." Dylan put his hands up. "Fucking small-ass town, can't keep nobody's business quiet."

"Look at this." My dad was off to the side of the room, but he gestured to the group. "The entire band shows up for you and you're still not going to go to New York?"

"What the fuck did he just say?" Dylan cocked one eyebrow at me, though he was pointing at Mickey. "Did he just say you're giving up New York?"

"I'll drag your ass there myself," Rock stated, crossing his arms over his chest. "That's fucking stupid."

Charlie punched me in the shoulder, hard. "Have you lost your damn mind?"

All of my friends began talking over one another, incredulous at my decision and balking at the stupidity of it all.

"Guys, guys! Damn! I'm going. Okay? I'm going." I looked my father square in the face, silently thanking him. "Dad, I'm going. You were right. I need to do this."

Mickey grinned. "Hell yes." He gave me a stiff hug, then headed back down the hallways toward my mother's room.

I turned back to my friends. "Guess I'm going to New York."

"New York, watch the fuck out!" Dylan cheered, heading toward the exit with the rest of the group following him.

"*Logan Clay* is going to be in lights!" Charlie announced. "Fucking lights, bro."

"You better get me front row tickets when you play Madison Square Garden!" Rock pumped his fist in the air. "And my pick of the groupies."

I laughed, ignoring their wisecracks. The realization was just sinking in, somehow for the first time. *Holy shit, I'm going to New York.*

## 10

"I came here once on a field trip, but all I remember is the zoo and Central Park," I said, wide-eyed, as Gina and I walked down the New York City sidewalk together early the next morning.

"It's wonderful, isn't it?" Gina smiled dreamily, stretching out her hands as if to hug the entire city. "New York has a charm that rivals none."

I was absolutely intoxicated with the look of pure love on her face right now. "What was it like growing up here?"

"Magical. It's in my blood," she said, taking his hand and squeezing it. "I only moved out by you for graduate school, but I always planned on coming back."

They entered the park, walking down the long paths until I suddenly decided to stop. Gina looked at me, confused, but I pulled her swiftly into my arms and held her tightly against my chest.

Leaning down, I kissed her softly. The taste of her lips and the feeling of her body pressed against mine fed my hunger, and I deepened our kiss, crushing her in my arms as she eagerly gave me what I wanted.

When I finally pulled away, I had no idea how much time had even passed.

"What was that for?" Gina sighed. We started walking again, still hand-in-hand.

"The look on your face just then." I smiled at her. "You love this city."

She sighed again. "Mmhm, I really do."

"One day, you're going to look at me like that," I said nonchalantly. "One day you're going to love me as much as I love you."

Gina suddenly slowed down. "Wait...what?"

I turned to her and let my fingers dance up her arm. "Do I need to repeat myself?"

"Fuck yes, you need to repeat yourself," she exclaimed. I could tell she was pretending to be annoyed even though I could see the light dancing in her eyes.

"I know it's soon, Gina. But I feel something here that I never felt before. A future. Excitement. Like you and I were always meant to be partners. I love you."

She swallowed hard, a panicked look beginning to creep on to her face. "We...we haven't even talked about a relationship or anything like that," she stuttered. "I don't know what to say..."

"Tell me you don't love me then." I cocked one brow and stared at her defiantly, daring her to lie.

She didn't reply, biting her lip. She glanced up at me, then away, then back again.

"Tell me you don't love me," I repeated slowly, closing the gap between them.

"Damn it." She let out a long exhale than flung her arms around my neck. She kissed me hard the moment my arms caught her. I lifted her off the ground, her feet dangling as my grip tightened. She brought her lips to my ear and whispered, "Don't you know by now that I never do what I'm told?"

I let out a loud laugh and squeezed her tighter. I kissed her lips, then the tip of her nose, both of her cheeks, and finally her forehead before I put her back on the ground.

Gina grabbed my hand and pulled me forward. "Come on. You're going to make yourself late at the pace we are going."

I quickly matched her pace, stealing a smile as we headed to the studio.

\* \* \*

"Ever been in a recording booth before, Logan?" Garrett asked as he ushered me into the control room of the studio.

Gina followed us in but stayed out of the way.

"No, sir. Never been to more than two places in this whole city," I admitted. It was strange that I had lived in New York all my life, but never been to the city. There'd never been much time or money for traveling with my mother's health.

"Get some sightseeing in while you're here," he replied. "You're Irish, right? Make your way up to Woodlawn in the Bronx, catch a fight at Legends. You'll have the time of your life."

"I'm not much of a fighter," I joked, though that was the truth.

Garrett laughed. "Yeah, I don't suppose so. Most artists are more the lover type."

I looked around the studio once more. The glass partition into the recording booth and the millions of buttons and levers all over that meant absolutely nothing to me, but I couldn't have been happier just being there.

Garrett pointed toward the door of the soundproof room. "We have a decent set up here, so I think you're going to sound great. Go on in and get comfortable. Take a seat, find your guitar, and when you're ready, we'll start recording."

I agreed, my nerves making me a little shaky. Gina squeezed my hand, giving me the extra boost I needed.

I quickly found my guitar, which had been brought in earlier, and brushed the sparkling red instrument with my fingertips. I smiled at the memory of every performance at McGinny's, every bedside song for my mother, and every garage band practice over the years.

Perching on a stool in front of the microphone, I pulled on the headphones dangling beside it. My guitar on one knee and a pick in my hand, I tested it out, strumming a few chords. I stopped to tune it, twisting the knobs at the top, then strummed again, listening carefully. After perfecting the sound, I gave a thumbs-up to Garrett who was on the other side of the glass partition beside Gina.

His voice came over the intercom. "When you see the red light above the window go on, it means we're recording. Got it?"

I nodded my understanding and then looked to the light. A few seconds later, it flashed on, and I played the first few chords to my favorite song.

*Stole my heart just to throw it away,*
    *No explanation for the games you play.*
    *Am I just a Friday night to you,*

*Or are we going to see this through?*

I COULD SEE Gina and Garrett talking while I sang, but I tried to pay it no attention. She was smiling so wide that it seemed promising.

*BETWEEN OUR KISSES, YOU SAID "FOREVER,"*
   *but behind my back, you laughed "never."*
   *So, I tossed the thief from my bed,*
   *but damn it all, you're still in my head.*

GARRETT LEANED DOWN, writing something on a small piece of paper. When he stood, I recognized it as a check. He handed it to Gina, and a smug look took up ownership on her face. She pocketed it and then shook her father's hand. Something edged at my senses, alarm bells off in the distance, but I pushed those aside.

*EVEN IF I lock up my whole heart,*
   *You pierce your way in like a dart,*
   *Now your reign of power's through,*
   *I'm not the one you'll come home to.*

GARRETT GAVE me a thumbs-up as I moved into the final chorus of the song. This was it. I was going to be signed with one of the biggest recording labels in town. I was going to be famous. I was going to be a star.

. . .

*Did you hear, girl, what I said?*
*No more damn thieves in my bed.*
*Did you hear, girl, what I said?*
*Get the fuck out of my bed!*


Garret voice came back over the loudspeaker. "That was it! Perfect, Logan. Put your equipment away and come join us."

I grinned, still feeling the surge of adrenaline from performing in a studio for the first time...and with such high stakes. I put up my guitar and then paused when I heard Gina's voice on the loudspeaker as well.

"Thanks, Dad. I knew I was a shoe-in to win when I heard him."

"My girl always was a competitor. The fifty-thousand-dollar bonus is yours, along with the job." I turned around to see Garrett shaking Gina's hand, then walking out of the studio. "Now, wait to break his heart until after he's signed the deal."

Still smiling, Gina turned back to look at me through the glass. I stood there, frozen. I wasn't even able to process everything I'd just heard. She reached for the loudspeaker button, seemingly to ask him what was wrong, but then did a double take. He watched as she realized that her father had accidentally left on the loudspeaker, and that I'd heard everything she'd just said.

I suddenly came to life and stormed toward the door to the booth, bursting into the control room, which was now empty except for Gina. I quickly closed the gap between us, anger coursing through my body as I found myself wondering if I'd just been played...or used...or hell, I didn't even know what was happening.

"What the fuck was that?" I seethed.

She shook her head, her hands out defensively. "It's not what it sounded like, I swear. I've always wanted to work here, but my dad wouldn't hire me until I proved I could do the job. It's just business, Logan."

"Not even two hours ago, I told you I loved you. Now you're telling me I was just a damn job to you? A fifty-thousand-dollar bonus?" I was getting angrier by the second, my large frame towering over her. "This was just about money?"

She scooted away to put a bit more distance between us. "That's not true. I mean, okay...at first it was. I heard your music and I knew you were my in to get this job, and the bonus."

"How could I have been so stupid?" I groaned and ran my fingers through my hair, walking toward the door. "Damn it, Gina. I thought we meant something to each other."

"Logan, don't go!" She grabbed my arm, stepping in front of me to block my exit. "It started out that way, but it's real for me now. I care about you, I want to be with you."

"You want to be with a meal ticket," I replied, moving around her.

She wrapped her arms around herself, like she was hugging herself. "Please, Logan...I love you."

I paused and tilted my head, looking down at her. I couldn't tell if she was lying or just saying what she thought I wanted to hear. Hell, I couldn't tell who she was at all anymore.

"If you really meant that, you would have said it in the park. Not now." With that, I walked out of the door and closed it behind me.

## 11

I stared at the bleak hospital wall over my mother's bed while she slept. I'd sent my father home for a few hours to shower and change since he had barely left her side, especially while I was gone.

I hadn't slept since my trip to New York the day before, and my eyes were burning with exhaustion. As much as I wanted to sleep, my brain was playing a cruel trick on me, replaying the fight with Gina again and again.

A tall, thin doctor with short blond hair walked into the room. He carried a tablet, scanning the screen as he walked. The long white doctor's coat over his blue scrubs was a bit rumpled, as though he'd napped in it. "Mr. Clay?"

"That's me." I turned and stood.

"Oh, I was looking for Mr. Mickey Clay?" The doctor looked surprised to see me answering.

I nodded. "That's my father. He stepped out for a few minutes," I explained. "How's she doing? Any news?"

His lips tightened into a flat line, then he shook his head. "There's nothing new with your mom's condition. We are still waiting for an available kidney."

"Oh." I mustered up after a moment of silence, uncertain what to say or what else to ask. It seemed we were just waiting, hoping our clock didn't run out before the solution arrived.

"Unfortunately, I am here on slightly different news," the doctor continued. "Your father's blood test was negative. We checked it again, like he asked, but he's definitely not a match."

"What are you talking about?" If my father was also sick, I wouldn't be able to handle it.

"He isn't a match to donate a kidney to your mother," the doctor clarified. "I am very sorry. I know how badly he wanted to be, but it's just not a viable option."

Hope sparked in me. "Test me," I demanded. "Please test me. Right now. Where do I go?"

"Well, hold on." The doctor put his hands up as if to stop me. "This isn't something to just jump into. There are risks in every procedure, especially something like this. If you're a match, it's something you'd really need to weigh."

"I don't care. Just test me," I replied. "The worst-case scenario is I'm not a match. So, let's find out."

The doctor shook his head. "The worst case scenario is you are a match, you donate your kidney, and then you end up in the same situation as your mother—or worse."

"What's going on?" Dylan walked into the hospital room, and his gaze flicked between the doctor and me.

Rock and Charlie appeared behind him and hovered in the doorway, arms across their chests, looking like bodyguards, ready to protect and defend.

"I want them to test my blood, see if I am a match to donate a kidney. Doc here doesn't think it's a good idea because I could be in the same predicament down the road," I explained quietly, gesturing to my mother who was still asleep. The pain medications she'd been given not too long ago had a strong sedative effect, and I was glad she wasn't awake to witness this because she'd have agreed with the doctor.

"Test mine, too," Dylan said, staring down the doctor.

"Me too." Rock announced.

"Right here," Charlie agreed, raising his hand to volunteer as well. "Let's do this."

The doctor smiled at all of us, clearly seeing we were serious. "Okay. We will test you all. However, if one of you is a match, we will need to carefully discuss the long-term consequences before we take the next step."

"Understood," Dylan said simply, as if it was not a big deal at all.

The rest of us agreed, and as I looked around the room, all I saw were determined faces of the men who were basically my brothers. There was no doubt on any of their faces, and my gratitude swelled.

"I'll send a nurse in to draw blood in a moment. Sit tight." Then the doctor left them alone in the room.

"You don't have to do this," I said, looking around at each of them. "None of you. This should be my responsibility. She's not your mother."

Dylan put his hand up. "First of all, the fuck she's not, asshole. That woman raised me a lot more than any other woman on this planet. Do you know where the fuck my mother is? Because I sure as shit don't."

"I didn't mean—" I tried to interrupt, realizing how rude I'd probably sounded.

"And second, fuck yeah. If you're a match, that kidney is coming out of you, not me. You can take that promise to the bank, kid." Dylan grinned and punched me on the left side of my chest.

"Jeez," I said, rubbing my chest.

Rock pointed at Dylan. "What he said. And have you ever had your momma's shepherd's pie? I'd give a lot more than one damn kidney to keep having that for the rest of my life."

"What do I need two kidneys for anyway?" Charlie added. "You bastards always make me be the fucking designated driver, so I'm certainly not using it as much as your drunk asses."

We all started laughing, but quickly realized we were going to wake my mother. Creeping out of the room, we reconvened in the hallway when my phone began buzzing in my pocket.

I pulled it out and glanced at the screen. Unknown number. "Hello?"

"Mr. Clay, this is Garrett Vile calling from New York New Music."

A knot formed in my stomach. "Uh, yes. Yes, sir. How can I help you?"

Vile cleared his throat. "You left so quickly yesterday. I didn't get to hear your answer."

"My answer to what?" I couldn't recall whatever Garrett was referring to.

"The recording contract, of course." Garrett sounded a bit irritated now. "Didn't Gina go over it with you?"

"Oh, uh...no. I didn't give her the chance to. My mother became ill, and I had to rush home," I said, covering for Gina. I didn't even know why I did it, honestly. It was just a gut reaction to protect her, despite how badly she'd hurt me. It was clear how much her father's approval meant to her just from the way she stared at him and everything she'd done to earn a spot in his company. That, at the very least, was a feeling he could relate to.

"Sorry to hear that, son. If you've got a minute, I can go over the terms with you right now..." he suggested.

"Um, sure." I motioned with excitement for my friends to come listen to the conversation. They huddled close to me on one side of the hospital hallway as I put the call on speakerphone and held the phone out so everyone could hear.

"The contract is for four years, renewable at the end of the term. A one million dollar advance to start, and then we split everything fifty-fifty. You will be required to do at least two full albums during that time. We will want to do a tour probably every other year, but there is some wiggle room on that. You will also get five percent of all ticket sales. Merchandise is ten percent. There are a lot more details, but those are the major highlights. How do you think that sounds?"

This would change my life. This would change everything.

I was feeling a little lightheaded and found a chair nearby to sit in as I wrapped my mind around everything I'd just heard.

Dylan's face was so ecstatic, he was almost jumping up and down. Charlie looked stunned, and Rock grinned like they had all just won the lottery. The overwhelming feeling of support laid heavy on my chest.

I owed these men for any musical success I would ever have. I was never going to forget that.

My mind slipped to Gina for a few moments, wishing she were here to share in this excitement. At least the Gina he had known and loved, not whoever the real version was. It had all been an act and yet here he was missing her.

"Well, Logan, how does that sound?" Garrett asked again, the barest hint of irritation coloring his voice.

I sat up abruptly, realizing I'd completely forgotten to reply in all the excitement. "It sounds amazing, sir. I'd love to sign."

"Good. Glad to have you on board. The lawyers will send over the paperwork shortly. Make sure to have your lawyer look it over and send it back. Once all that is squared away, New York New Music will officially become your representative," he concluded.

"Thank you, sir. This is amazing news," I gushed, unable to hold back my eagerness.

My friends were high-fiving one another and smacking me on the back in triumph.

"Get ready to be a star, Logan Clay," Garrett said as he hung up.

"Congrats, Logan. That's freaking amazing," Rock said.

"Fuck yes, man!" Dylan cheered they all headed back into the hospital room with huge smiles on their faces.

I stood in the hallway a moment longer, trying to find the feeling in my legs again after everything I'd just heard.

A sniffling sound to my right caught my attention. I turned to see a young girl slumped down in her chair. She was maybe two or three years younger than me with dark brown, wavy hair falling over her face.

"Are you okay, miss?" I asked awkwardly, taking a few steps closer.

She waved her hands as if to tell him to not worry about her. "I'm fine. Don't let me bother you."

I paused and looked back toward my mother's hospital room. I could hear her voice and my band mates, happily celebrating the news.

Biting back the urge to run from anything unpleasant, I walked over to the mystery woman. Something about her seemed so innocent, so in need. "What's got you so upset?"

"I'm not upset," she said, a deep blush creeping up her cheeks. "These are actually happy tears."

I smiled, because I definitely could understand that, especially now.

She looked up at me when I didn't reply, and her bright hazel eyes pierced through me so hard I almost lost my breath. "You must think I'm pretty weird."

"No," I assured her. "I get it. I got some good news today, too."

She nodded, a smile creeping on to her lips. "You could say that. One of my best friends had a terrible skiing accident a while back and today was the first time she walked again on her own."

I reached out and squeezed her forearm. "That's amazing. Congratulations."

"Thanks," she said. "What about you? What's your news?"

I paused, unsure what to say. It seemed odd to say I just earned a million-dollar paycheck. "I got the job I was applying for."

"Oh, my goodness!" She stood up and wrapped me in an impromptu hug. I froze for a moment, not prepared for the sudden burst of affection from a stranger. "That must be so exciting. A whole new start to your life."

"Thanks," I said, faltering.

I studied her expression, looking for hints of sarcasm or something negative, but there was nothing. This complete stranger was going through something much more important than my music career, yet she was genuinely ecstatic for me.

I wondered if Gina would ever be that kind of person. Someone who would genuinely feel for other people when her own ambitions weren't on the line. She'd helped him with his career, that was certain, but had it been because she liked him and his music? Or had it been for her own career gains?

But this woman? This was the kind of person he wanted to be around. A sweet and selfless person who would stop to chat with a stranger.

"Well, thanks again, uh..." I realized I'd never gotten her name.

"Caroline," she replied. "I've got to get going, but congrats again!" With that, she walked off and turned the next corner.

I watched her for a moment, enjoying the warmth in my whole body at such a positive encounter and wondering if I'd judged Gina too quickly. Maybe she could be that type of person, and I'd just never given her the chance.

\* \* \*

"I REALLY WISH you boys talked to me before you did that." My mother sighed and rubbed her fists over her eyes.

"You would've just said no," I replied from where I was sitting at the foot of her bed. My band mates were all crowded into the hospital room as well, and my father was in the chair next to the bed. It had been almost twenty-four hours since we'd had our blood drawn and had been told we'd receive the news any minute now.

"Damn right she would have said no," Mickey grumbled and glared at all of us. "And I would have agreed with her."

"Momma Clay, you don't need to worry about any of us," Rock said, a softness in his voice that I'd rarely heard. "We are not the little boys that ran around your backyard playing all day anymore."

"We are all smart and edu-ma-cated now," Charlie slowly, purposely mispronounced the word.

She grinned at us, tears flooding her eyes. "You may be all grown up now—and three or four times my size—but you will always be my boys."

Mickey rolled his eyes and grumbled something inaudible, which caused all of us to burst out laughing.

"Are we celebrating something in here?" A nurse smiled as she waltzed in and picked up the clipboard hanging at the end of my mother's bed.

"My boys are just teasing me," my mother replied, shaking a finger at us.

"They are all your sons? Man, you must have had your hands full back in the day." The nurse chuckled as she wrote in the chart.

"Every single one of them." Mom grinned at us and we all nodded in agreement.

"Well, you have a beautiful family, ma'am," the nurse replied as she headed for the exit. "Your doctor is over in the next room finishing up, so he'll be here soon."

"We should have told her that the real celebration is Logan." Rock pointed at me. "Soon, we can all say that we know a celebrity!"

I rolled my eyes.

"Plus, we'll have the hook up to front row tickets for the hottest shows in town!" Dylan added.

"It's a record deal. That doesn't mean I'll become famous," I cautioned with a self-conscious chuckle.

"The fuck it doesn't!" Rock said. "You are going to make over seven fucking figures this year alone!"

"Hey, watch your mouth around a lady!" Mickey abruptly cut in.

Rock put his hands up and mouthed *I'm sorry* to my mother, who was laughing.

I decided to play into their joke, even though there was a far chance in hell that I'd ever be actually famous. "I can tell you now that the moment I get my first check, Mom, you're getting out of this place. The nicest hospital suite we can find, with at least six windows. And room service. Maybe a butler."

"What do I need a butler for?" Laura laughed again. "Oh, Logan. I knew you could do it."

"We all knew he could do it. It was convincing him that was the problem," Dylan said.

"Never a doubt in my mind," Mickey said quietly.

The entire room went silent and looked at him. It wasn't often that you heard a compliment from Mickey Clay and I was soaking in every syllable.

"Knock, knock," the same doctor from yesterday said awkwardly, standing in the door wearing the same scrubs and coat.

"Come on in, doctor!" Laura said.

He walked in hesitantly and looked down at his tablet. "I've got good news and bad news."

"Let's hear it," I said, eager to find out if I was a match.

The doctor nodded, then looked back down at the tablet. "We tested Mickey's blood the other day and it wasn't a match. We tested all four of you and unfortunately, none of you were a match either."

Rock's jaw dropped. "None of us?"

"Out of everyone here, not a single person was viable?" Charlie was incredulous.

I looked silently at the doctor, my jaw rigid with tension.

I heard my mother let out a quiet sigh and I reached over to squeeze her hand.

"You said you had good news, doctor. But so far, all I heard was a ton of shit," Mickey said loudly.

Everyone turned to look at Mickey and then back at the doctor, awaiting his response.

"Yes, there was one match," he replied. "So, that's great news. She has already signed all the paperwork, agreeing to the donation. We can do the surgery right now if you are ready, Laura."

What the hell?

"You just said there *wasn't* a match." I furrowed my brow and tried to understand what the doctor was saying.

"None of you were a match, but your friend was. A, uh —" He clicked a few buttons on the tablet, then came up with a name. "Gina Vile. She was a match and is being prepped now."

"I don't know who that person is," my mother replied in confusion.

I stood up straight, my heart beating a million beats a minute. "Gina?"

Dylan stepped forward. "Wait, Logan's girl?"

"Wow, I didn't know she got tested," Charlie said slowly.

"You have a girlfriend, Logan?" Mickey was now standing and the entire room was firing questions back and forth in utter chaos.

"Everyone, stop!" I shouted and the room fell silent.

The doctor cleared his throat. "I'm going to go. If you want to see Ms. Vile, she is being prepped in Pre-Op 3." The doctor looked uncomfortable and backed out of the room quickly.

Everyone's eyes turned to me, but I was still trying to sort out everything that I had just heard.

"So, your girlfriend wants to donate a kidney to me? Why didn't we even know you had a girlfriend?" My mother broke the silence quietly, speaking slowly.

"I broke up with her in New York," I tried to explain. "She wasn't honest about who she was, she only started dating me to convince me to take the record deal."

"Didn't you already want the record deal?" Charlie asked, crossing his arms over his chest.

"Yeah, of course," Logan replied.

"Then what convincing did she need to do?" Dylan asked, poking holes in my logic and making me think back on my time with her.

"Did you guys only talk about the record deal?" Rock asked. "Because you were a different person around her. You seemed so happy."

"Not really. Not seriously anyway," I admitted.

"Then why did you break up with her?" my father chimed in.

I hung my head and sighed. All of my reasons weren't making sense anymore, or they just didn't seem as important. So, she'd wanted a job. She'd wanted him to succeed. She'd wanted to prove herself to her father. Could he really fault her that?

"Shit," I muttered.

"Logan, go talk to her, baby," my mother said. "But for God's sake, do not let this woman give me her kidney. I never even met her and my son has been a complete ass to her."

## 12

---

When I spotted her, she was sitting on the edge of an examination table in one of the standard gowns. Her colorful hair was tied back into a braid and she wasn't wearing a stitch of makeup, yet she looked as beautiful as she always had. She was talking to the nurses, worry clearly etched on her face, but there was something else, too. Determination. Resolve.

This wasn't going to be an easy fight.

"Can I have a moment alone with her, please?" I asked of the nurse when I stepped into the room.

Gina's head snapped up and her eyes landed on me.

"Sure. We can spare a couple of minutes," the nurse said, motioning for the other orderlies and nurses to leave. Within moments, they were alone.

"What are you doing here?" Gina asked softly, looking down at her feet in thick hospital socks dangling off the side of the table.

"What am *I* doing here? Gina...what's going on?" I walked over to the side of the table, my arms crossing over my chest as I pushed my shoulders back.

Her swallow was visible on her throat. "I didn't know that you would find out. I'm sorry."

I frowned, surprised at how anguished she looked. She seemed to be pouring out emotion when I'd rarely ever seen this side of her. "Do you think I'm suddenly going to forget everything you did and be with you if you do this? Do you think it'll sweeten the record deal or something?"

She looked startled, her eyes widening for a moment then falling into a wounded look he immediately felt guilty for causing. "Of course not! I didn't even know they would tell you my name."

"You're doing this...with no ulterior motive?" I asked again, softer this time.

She sighed. "Does it matter?"

"I can't think of anything in my life that has \ mattered more." I dropped my arms to my side and looked at her. "I'm surprised you don't know that."

She furrowed her brow as she stared at him. "What are you talking about?"

I closed the distance between us with a few small steps. Pushing her legs apart, I stood between her knees against the table. I placed my hands flat on the padded surface on either side of her and leaned closer, only inches from her face.

"You matter to me, Gina," I whispered softly, causing her eyes to dart up and meet mine.

"Really?" she choked out, clearly pushing back tears. My heart ached at the realization that she didn't know that, and that that was my fault. I'd given her my love and then taken it back so swiftly. She deserved more than that after all she'd done for me.

I leaned down and kissed the tear off her cheek, then wrapped my arms around her back and pulled her tighter against me. She hugged her legs around my waist, her hands on the back of my neck.

"Really, Gina," I confirmed, kissing her jaw and whispering in her ear.

She buried her face in my neck, inhaling deeply. "I love you, Logan," she whispered, slightly muffled, into his skin.

I chuckled and kissed her cheek. "I know."

She pulled back to look at me, a hesitant grin tugging at her lips. "How do you know?"

"That look on your face," I replied, kissing her softly. "It's the same look you gave New York. I told you you'd look at me like that one day."

She scrunched up her nose and defiantly stuck out her tongue.

A loud burst of laughter escaped from me, my head tilted back until I'd calmed down. I kissed her hard this time, devouring her mouth as she leaned into me. Her hospital gown split in the back and I slid my hands inside, pulling her closer to the table's edge.

Her breathing was ragged. "Logan," she gasped as I slid my hand to between her legs, pushing beneath her underwear. "We can't do this here! What if someone sees us?"

"We'll charge them for tickets later." I teased, pressing one finger into her.

She groaned and her body fell forward into mine. "But, I'm about to have surgery," she continued to protest even though she was sounding less and less convincing with each stroke of my finger.

"The hell you are." I said firmly, stroking across her and pressing her clit in a way that made her jolt. "You're not doing that."

"Don't you know by now that I never do what I'm told?" she whispered into my ear seductively.

"You're going to be the death of me, woman." I growled, gently nipping her skin as I plunged another finger inside her.

I wouldn't know for a few more years how true my last words were.

# EPILOGUE

## 2012

"I heard you the first time, Gina."

"And yet, you're just standing there not getting ready." She folded her arms over her chest and tapped her high heel against the marble floor of our New York City penthouse.

Logan placed his hand against the glass, leaning against it as he looked out onto the city. "I have two hours. I planned on checking in on my mom first," he said, turning and walking past her into the bedroom to grab his cell phone.

"You spoke to her this morning," Gina called after him, then stomped to the kitchen. "I have one kidney, too, you know. It would be really nice if you could fucking act like I am just as important."

He rolled his eyes and took a deep breath, dialing his parent's house.

"Hi, honey," my mother's voice chimed through the phone.

"Hey, Mom. How are you feeling today?"

"Baby, you don't need to keep checking on me. I'm fine, perfectly healthy," she assured him. "That nurse you hired is so sweet, and she takes good care of me. Your dad is loving his new job. Just having somewhere to go every day helps him, I think."

"I know it's been a few years since the transplant, but I worry about you." He sighed. "I feel like I never get to talk to you anymore."

"I know, baby. I miss you, too, but I understand," she said. "I see you on the entertainment news all the time. You're playing so many shows. I'm so proud of you, honey."

"Thanks, Mom."

"How is my beautiful Gina?" she asked next.

"She's fine. She says hello," Logan lied, pacing back and forth around the bedroom. He hated lying to his mother, but he didn't want her to know how things really were. Not after everything they'd been through.

"Mom, I gotta go," Logan said. "I have a show tonight, need to dress and go to sound check. Give my love to Dad, okay?"

"Of course, baby boy," she replied, then she paused for a moment. "Hey, Logan? Maybe try to come out to see us sometime soon? It's been so long."

"I'll look at my schedule, Mom. Soon, I hope. Okay? Love you." He hung up and tossed his phone onto the bed.

He pulled his shirt off and headed to his walk-in closet. His jaw was tight and he could feel the bitterness coursing through him as he slid clothes around on the rack, deciding what to wear. Finally picking some tight black jeans and a leather top, he got dressed and headed out into the living room.

Gina stood at the kitchen island. She was tapping away on her laptop, a serious look on her face. Her jet-black hair was pulled up into a tight bun. The colorful streaks that had once fascinated Logan were long gone, and she was wearing a navy pencil skirt and linen blouse over a pair of stilettos.

As he walked in, she glanced up at him and then let out an exasperated sigh. "What the hell are you wearing?"

"What do you mean?" Logan stopped in his tracks, looking down at his outfit.

"I put the outfit for tonight on the back of the closet door. Can you please go put that one on? We really don't have time for this." She went back to typing.

"This outfit is fine," he replied. "I'm wearing this."

"Seriously?" Gina's heels clicked across the floor as she walked over to him, her hands on her hips. "Who is your manager, Logan? Who made you the star that you are today? Was it you? Was it your mom? No, it was *me*. So, if I say to wear a different outfit, don't you think I have some inkling as to what I am talking about?"

"I'm not an idiot, Gina. I can pick my own damn shirt."

Gina changed tactics, and he could see it coming before she even said it. "Can you *please* just go change? Don't you think you owe me at least that for everything I've given up?" Gina gestured to her side.

Logan followed her hands and thought of the large scar on her back beneath her blouse and all that it implied. He sighed, feeling guilty, and headed back toward the bedroom.

He wouldn't change his past for anything, because his mother was alive and healthy. But it had come with a heavy cost.

# ABOUT THE AUTHOR

*Photo Credit: Valerie Bey*

**Sarah Robinson** is the Top 10 Barnes & Noble and Amazon Bestselling Author of multiple series and standalone novels, including the *Exposed* series, *The Photographer Trilogy*, *Kavanagh Legends* series, the *Forbidden Rockers* series, and *Not a Hero: A Marine Romance*. A native of Washington, D.C., Robinson has both her bachelor's and master's degrees in forensic and clinical psychology and works as a counselor. She owns a small zoo of furry pets and is actively involved in volunteering in her community.

## ALSO BY SARAH ROBINSON

**The Photographer Trilogy**

*(Romantic Suspense)*

Tainted Bodies

Tainted Pictures

Untainted

The Photographer Trilogy Boxset

**Forbidden Rockers Series**

*(Rockstar Romances)*

Her Forbidden Rockstar

Rocker Christmas: A Logan & Caroline Holiday Novella

Logan's Story: A Prequel Novella

Logan Clay: The Box Set

**Kavanagh Legends Series**

*(MMA Fighter Standalone Romances)*

Breaking a Legend

Saving a Legend

Becoming a Legend

Chasing a Legend

Kavanagh Christmas

**EXPOSED Series**

*(Hollywood Standalone Romances)*

NUDES

BARE

SHEER

Exposed Boxed Set

**100 Proof Series**

*(Contemporary Country Romances)*

Wylde Fire *(Coming 2019)*

Wylde Spirits *(Coming 2020)*

Wylde Hearts *(Coming 2020)*

**Standalone Novels**

Not a Hero: A Bad Boy Marine Romance

Misadventures with a Cage Fighter *(Coming 2020)*

Made in the USA
Middletown, DE
31 May 2019